The Drowning Eyes

D0030192

THE

DROWNING

EYES

Emily Foster

A TOM DOHERTY ASSOCIATES BOOK

NEW YORK

This is a work of fiction. All of the characters, organizations, and events portrayed in this novella are either products of the author's imagination or are used fictitiously.

THE DROWNING EYES

Copyright © 2016 by Emily Foster
Map copyright © 2015 by Tim Paul

Cover art by Cynthia Sheppard
Cover design by Christine Foltzer
Edited by Carl Engle-Laird

All rights reserved.

A Tor.com Book
Published by Tom Doherty Associates, LLC
175 Fifth Avenue
New York, NY 10010

www.tor.com

Tor® is a registered trademark of Tom Doherty Associates, LLC.

ISBN 978-1-4668-9193-7 (e-book)
ISBN 978-0-7653-8768-4 (trade paperback)

First Edition: January 2016

For Suzanne, who asked about the maps on my wall

The Long Banks

to Chândragûn

Moliki

Kuhon

Jepjep

Jena Prefecture

Humma

to Caddria

The Jihiri Islands

Tash

Dos Mijari

The Drowning Eyes

Chapter 1

"Not in *this* lifetime." Tazir snatched two of the pebbles off of the pile for the equipment budget. "Or at least not after what you pulled coming into Hanshi."

Her hatchet-nosed quartermaster locked her amber eyes on Tazir's. "I told you, Cap, just because I *can* hack that together in a pinch don't mean I plan on doing it every—"

"And how are we not in a pinch?" Tazir asked, dropping the pebbles back on the greasy wooden bartop with the rest of the pile for food.

Chaqal opened her mouth to say something, but Tazir could see her eyes taking in the scene around them. Young as Chaqal was, she had the good sense to be leery of this place—not so much an inn as a dockside canopy set up above a stack of rum barrels and the square bar surrounding them.

It had shade, and it had rum, and in the evenings it had a couple ribby dancers who came around to rub up against the customers—but ah, the customers. Whether tall and sinewy or short and ham-legged, whether

9

adorned with tattoos or deliberate scars, whether trained with a hook-head spear or a Bahenji swinging club, the customers were bad news. It didn't matter if they belonged to a tribe or an island or were just a merchant Captain with a lot of cash to drop on security. Unless you were talking to a dancer, the barkeep, or someone you knew, you kept your eyes down and your elbows in tight while you were drinking at Shasa's.

Chaqal glared at her little pile. "Can I just get one more dak?" she asked.

Tazir's eyebrows sank together. "Can you just eat a little less?"

On Tazir's other side, her first mate cleared his throat. "If it helps," he said, "I'm inclined to give her both dakki and count on this passenger for the rest of your food money."

"Dammit, Kodin," Tazir said, rubbing her weathered forehead. "Look, we have no idea if we'll even *find* anyone." It had been her idea, coming to Shasa's to pick up one of the travelers who came through looking for a cheap ride who didn't ask too many questions. Last time she was in this place, it had been buzzing with "runaway bride" and "looking for my brother" and even the odd, honest, "I killed someone back in my hometown and I need to get halfway across the ocean as fast as I can."

But last time had been almost a year ago, and nobody

had even heard of the Dragon Ships back then. Since last time, Shasa's had been gripped by the same fear and paranoia that was keeping the *Giggling Goat* out of her usual fishing grounds. No one—neither the goldsmiths of Luraina nor the blind weather witches of Tash—was safe from the vicious raiders in their fast ships, which meant that precious few people wanted to go anywhere. The ones who did preferred to travel with the most imposing and warlike crew they could find.

Now, although Tazir was deceptively strong and weathered by the sun and sea, she was just a little over five feet tall and slightly built. When it came to "imposing and warlike-looking," she just wasn't going to outdo the tall glowering women three seats down with intricate scars cascading down their broad shoulders and powerful legs. Or the trio of boulder-shaped Gurni men at the other corner, eyeing the crowd for passengers as blatantly as she and her crew were.

Chaqal could actually fight like a demon, but she looked even less warlike than Tazir. With big bovine eyes and plump, round lips, she still looked fifteen seven years after the fact. It didn't help that she liked to wear a long, flowing skirt and a tunic printed with flowers when she wasn't on the boat.

Of the three of them, Kodin looked the most useful in a fight. In fact, it was because of Kodin that their presence went unquestioned in Shasa's—he used to do security with someone's brother, who fought in a war down south with someone else's cousin, and so on and so forth. From what Tazir knew, he'd been good at security. He certainly looked the part. Tall and wide, with big square shoulders and big square fists, Kodin was built to make people cooperate. Even now that his fighting days were (mostly) done and his bushy beard was starting to show white, all it took was a stern look from him to get most people to quiet down.

Together, the three of them were mean enough that they'd had travelers rely on their protection in a pinch when they needed safe passage from one place to another. But, again, the last time that had happened, the Dragon Ships had not yet appeared on anybody's horizon. Now that they'd hit storm temples on Vura and Tash, everything had gotten a little bit harder.

"We should go somewhere else," Chaqal said, looking around. "In here, we look more like passengers ourselves."

"We won't be better off," Kodin said. "Those guys who left were saying the wind is shut down from Kahiri to Nua'ali."

Tazir shut her eyes for a moment, thinking of the havoc that was going to cause. "Perfect," she said. "The Dragon Ships don't need to bother burning our ports anymore—just scare us all until we lock ourselves in and starve to death."

"It's not that bad," Chaqal said.

"I don't know." Kodin flattened his lips. "Last time the Windspeakers shut down that much water, it started all kinds of trouble—fighting, riots, all the shit bored people do when they run out of money."

"But they can't just—just shut down *all* the wind," Chaqal asked. "Can they?"

"I guess sometimes," Tazir said, "when things are bad enough. Like last time, they had that bleeding fever over on Nderema, and they calmed the water for twenty miles in every direction until it was gone."

"When I was a kid," Kodin said, "we had these three pirate boats just wrecking people all over the place for no reason. Nobody could catch them until a Lurainese Shadowguard saw them in Luraina's waters. The Windspeakers had to shut down the entire island to give the Shadowguards a chance."

"Is that what they're trying with the dragon boats?" Chaqal asked. Instead of answering, Kodin picked up his wooden cup. He glared straight ahead as he drank the thick black rum inside, and Chaqal kept nursing her own drink. "Anyway," she said to Tazir. "I'd worry a lot less if I had a little more money to throw at repairs."

"I'll give you one more dak," Tazir said. "But if we run

out of money next time we make port, *you're* dancing on the tables."

"Hey, that means we're going somewhere nice, right?" Chaqal laughed, raucous barks of joy that seemed too big for her frame. "Yeah, fine, I'll take the one dak and stop pestering you. For now."

"Like you could just stop." Tazir plunked the pebble from the food budget back on the equipment budget. "Hey, Kodin," she said. "You want to write this down?"

The first mate dug in one of the pockets inside his embroidered vest until he found his tablet. He spit on his thumb and rubbed a corner clean, then started copying the budget down with the urba shell stylus tied to another corner.

"You're final on seven dakki for bribes?"

"I hope so," Tazir said. The Dragon Ships hadn't driven the cost of doing business up *that* high, but she was certain she'd find some port officer who disagreed.

Kodin finished copying the budget and snapped the tablet's leather cover shut again. "We've been tighter," he said.

"Yeah?" Tazir snorted, and spit on the ground. "When we had Mati on board, maybe."

"Maybe." Kodin gave her a halfhearted nod. "She *did* like her white wine."

Tazir shook her head and knocked on the bar for another drink. "The shit I did for that woman," she muttered at her knuckles. White wine, and a fortune's worth of it—now *that* was a way to remember a marriage. "Feh. It doesn't—"

"Hey," Chaqal said. She tapped Tazir on the shoulder and pointed to her right. "Coming down the dock. In the green."

Tazir turned her head to see who Chaqal was talking about. It didn't take her long. Tall and gangly, in a long skirt and short blouse of fine green silk, the kid stuck out like a sore thumb among the sailors and sellers who crowded Humma's spiderweb of docks. She wore her wiry black curls cropped close to her head like Mati used to. She was walking with her shoulders pinned together behind her back, and her eyes' frantic back-and-forth betrayed the calm on her pretty round face.

"Jingle, jingle, jingle," Tazir said to Kodin.

He grunted with laughter, then turned to her with a jerk. "Wait," he said. "You're serious?"

Tazir was already straightening her creaky hips as she stood on the dock. "I'll be back," she said. "With company."

"Captain, I'd bet money another crew's already—"

Tazir laughed and swaggered down the dock toward the girl. "Excuse me, ma'am," she said, holding her hand up as she approached. The girl stopped. A man walked right into her from behind and swore loudly in Djahrna.

"Sorry," the kid said, turning around and pulling her skirt out of his way as he picked up a bundle he'd dropped.

"Don't know where the *fuck* you think you from, girl—"

The girl's face darkened with embarrassment as the man made his way down the dock.

"Excuse me," Tazir repeated, stepping up to the girl and tugging at the sleeve of her blouse. "Are you looking for Shasa's?"

She flinched and pulled back, but her eyes brightened at the word. "Maybe," she said. "Someone told me there was a bar here where sailors wait for passengers?"

"That would be Shasa's," Tazir said. "Come on in—I'll buy you a drink."

She tried to link elbows with the girl, but the girl pulled away. Not surprising behavior in a rich kid like that, Tazir supposed—and judging by the feel of the silk, she was *real* rich.

"Oh. Uh, sorry, I—uh—" The girl flapped her mouth for a few moments like a fish in a net; her cheeks grew even darker.

"Don't worry about it." Tazir chuckled and tucked a stray braid back behind her ear. "I'm Tazir, by the way," she said.

"I'm Shina." The girl gave her a weak smile. Her eyes kept darting to the grimy shade of Shasa's Bar, and her eyebrows kept getting higher and higher on her forehead. "Is that—"

"Only the finest dockside drinking pit in Humma," Tazir said, gesturing toward Kodin and Chaqal with a flourish. "There you see my first mate and my quartermaster."

"Are you here looking for passengers?" The girl stopped and looked Tazir in the eye, her brows arched.

Tazir cocked her head to one side and rubbed her neck. "Well," she said, drawing the word out. "I mean, plenty of people come through looking for passage, but obviously we can't just take anyone who—"

"What if it was someone, uh, really clean and quiet?" Shina clasped her hands together. Her eyes were darting between the bar, Tazir's face, and the ground. "Who doesn't eat much?"

"This someone you know?" Tazir said, raising one brow.

"I, uh." The girl chewed on her cheek for a moment. "I was actually hoping to get passage myself," she said. "I—well, it's—"

Tazir looked the girl up and down, frowning just severely enough to make her afraid that someone was going to *disapprove*. Rich girls *hated* thinking that someone was going to *disapprove* of them—her marriage had at least taught her that much.

"Well," she said after a few moments, "let's discuss it."

Shina nodded; a smile flickered across her face. "Thanks," she said. Tazir watched the girl in backward glances as she followed her beneath the canopy of Shasa's. Her shoulders curled in around her chest like a turtle's shell. Her eyes were saucers, darting to all the thick, scarred faces in the shade.

"Hey-ey," Chaqal said. "Keep your eyes down, girl." She gave Tazir the steely, tight-mouthed glare that she *swore* she hadn't practiced in a mirror. "What does she want?"

"Says she wants passage somewhere," Tazir said. "Her name's Shina."

Shina swallowed, staring at the ground between her feet. She wore cheap, crudely made shoes—probably didn't want to get her embroidered slippers all covered in poor dust. "My parents are making me get married to this cousin of mine," she said. "I just can't *stand* him, but they're set on it."

Tazir met Kodin's eyes. Somebody had told this Shina girl what to say when she got to Shasa's.

"All right," Chaqal said. "They sending anybody after you?"

"I—I don't know," Shina said. "They might."

Tazir and Kodin looked each other in the eye again. All things considered, it wasn't unusual for a passenger to ask that they be ready to leave at any given moment. Depending on how dumb the passenger was, this could be a minor inconvenience or a major hazard.

"Where you planning on running to?" Chaqal asked.

"North." For once, the girl sounded sure of something. "Doesn't so much matter where in the north, just—I mean, I have a sister in Jepjep, so I need to see *her*, but north of Jepjep, at least—"

"We can do Jepjep," Kodin said. "We can do north, too—we've been up as far as the long banks."

"Pricey voyage," Tazir pointed out. "Could take months."

"I have plenty of money," Shina said. "I'll give you—"

"Hush, sweetheart," Chaqal said. "This isn't the place to go into detail about that kind of thing."

It was too late. The girl's voice had caught the attention of everyone in Shasa's. Nobody got up yet, but eyes swiveled over to look at this gangly, awkward rich kid.

Tazir looked at Kodin again. One corner of his mouth twitched downward, and he took in a deep breath. There was no denying that this could be a risky job—dumb passenger, no plan, maybe being chased by someone. There was also no denying that this could be their last chance today to generate some cash.

Chaqal raised her hand and waited for the barkeep to acknowledge her. "Let's talk about this some more out on the long docks," she said to Shina with a sweet smile. "It would be wonderful to have someone my age on board for a while—sailing with these two grumps got old a while ago."

The barkeep shuffled over with a tablet. "Two dakki," he said to Chaqal.

"Got it," she replied, reaching up beneath her linen tunic to get her coins from her purse. She dropped them in the barkeep's waiting palm and hopped off her stool.

Tazir and Kodin followed suit. Shina followed them out of the bar, and would have stuck to the rear of the group if Chaqal hadn't grabbed her by the wrist and shoved her forward.

"Be casual," she said with another one of those practiced cheerful grins. "It's a beautiful day, after all!" She wasn't entirely blowing smoke on that one. The wind hadn't yet been shut down in this part of the Jihiri Islands, and rolls of puffy white clouds gave the people a nice break from the sun now and then.

Shina opened her mouth, but then it seemed to dawn on her that she'd loudly told a bar full of big, crusty people that she was carrying plenty of money. She clamped her lips shut and picked up her pace. Behind them, the crowd was too thick to tell if anybody had followed them out of the bar.

"So," Tazir said. "Where are you from?"

"Nijia," the girl replied.

"Isn't that down east?"

"It's more south than east of here," the girl said with a casual shrug. "My parents have some sugar fields."

That took care of Tazir's next question. She steered the girl a little to the right, over onto one of the seven docks that extended into the Bay of Humma. The *Giggling Goat* was moored out there a few hundred yards.

"When did you leave home?" asked Kodin.

"Four days ago—no, five," Shina said. "They said I was going to start losing track of time."

"Who said?"

"The sailors on the ship I took from Nijia," she said. "They were nice—merchants, from Haresh."

"Yeah?" Tazir asked. She cocked her head to one side. "What was wrong with their ship?"

"Their master doesn't want them north of here," Shina said. "He—I didn't want to spend too much time talking to someone who might know my parents."

"Fair enough," Chaqal said.

That part of the story was probably more or less true. In Tazir's experience, rich people all tended to know each other intimately so that they could hate each other more completely.

The crowd was thinning out now, a couple hundred feet offshore. The dock was getting thinner, too, but that didn't stop the net repairers and fruit ice hawkers from setting up little boats full of wares they could sell to the sailors who were too hung over to make it all the way to the hub.

"How much money do you want?" Shina asked, finally hushing her voice. "I don't want to be rude, but—"

"Depends on how far you want us to go." Tazir pulled her pipe from a fold in the sash she wore around her waist.

"How far will you take me for forty thousand qyda?" Shina asked.

Tazir's hand stopped in the middle of loading the pipe with tobacco. "What?"

"I have forty thousand qyda," Shina said. "How far will it get me?"

Chaqal looked at Tazir. Tazir looked at Kodin. Kodin was grinning from ear to ear. Now, Tazir wasn't the world's best with exchange rates, but she remembered that a qyda was worth somewhere between six and ten dakki. Forty thousand was—was more money than she was going to see in one place ever again.

"That'll get you to the long banks," Kodin said. "Hell, if I'm in a good mood, it might even get you back."

"So you'll do it?" Shina said. "You'll take me north?"

Her eyebrows shot up her forehead, an excited grin tugging on the corners of her lips.

"Sure." Chaqal laughed. "But don't you want to see the boat first?"

Chapter 2

The *Giggling Goat* was a fifty-foot dhow that had been built some twenty or thirty years ago when shipbuilders had been in love with those deep, narrow hulls that could really power through rough water. It wasn't a terrible design for a fishing boat, all things considered, but that *rudder*—

Shina took in a deep breath and straightened her shoulders. *Rich and stupid,* she repeated to herself. *I am rich, and I am stupid. And rich. I am very, very rich.*

"—now, as you can see, we don't insist on privacy amongst ourselves." The quartermaster, a cheerful and ungainly girl who looked a few years older than her, was showing her the little nook they used as quarters. Everyone slept in one of the canvas hammocks that hung between the port hull and the center beam, so saturated with sweat and dirt and salt that they held the general shape of an ass.

"Oh," Shina said, blinking rapidly at the little dormitory. It wasn't much worse than the sleeping quarters at school, and it was far better than the cramped hold she'd huddled in while Dahas had burned behind her. *The last one,* she reminded herself. *I'm the last one.* She tried to ignore all the responsibility that entailed.

"Now, what I was thinking," the quartermaster said, "was while the hold is empty, we can set up some sheets or something and make a little dressing room for you. I think we still got a spare comb lying around here, even." She got on her hands and knees to crawl beneath the hammocks to the very back of the ship. "The Captain's ex-wife left a bunch of pretty stuff when they fell out—"

Shina's eyebrows shot up. "Oh—oh, you don't have to," she said, leaning down to watch the quartermaster rifling through sacks and trunks that had been tied to the rear of the hold. "I grew up with brothers."

The quartermaster rolled back out from under the hammocks. "Eh?" she said.

"It's all right," Shina said with a smile. "I grew up with lots of brothers and sisters—I don't mind close quarters."

"Oh." The quartermaster's face fell a little bit—had she been looking forward to setting up something nice? "Well, the Captain will like that, I guess."

Shina smiled. "I didn't mean to offend—"

"Oh, no," said the quartermaster. "Trust me, I do this to everybody." She laughed and brushed her knees off. "The Captain says I should've been an innkeep, the way I go on." She'd changed from the pretty blue-and-yellow tunic and trousers into a more practical outfit of red-and-brown linen. Her hair was long and straight, and she wore it in a thick braid down her muscular back. She was prettiest when she smiled, and Shina liked that she laughed loudly and often.

"Maybe that's why you're the quartermaster," Shina said.

"Nah, that's because I'm a good kisser." She grinned and stepped to the other side of the hold. "Anyway, here's where we store luggage—if you've got someone bringing your bags, you can just have him leave them topside and we'll stow them down here."

"I don't have any bags," Shina said. "I mean I—I had to leave in a hurry." She took a deep breath, tried to wall the memory out of her mind. She didn't have time for it now—but still, she could feel the old fear starting to heat her blood.

"Fair enough," said the quartermaster. She rapped on a board that had been strapped to the wall. "Now this," she said, "is the kitchen—you let the table down and put your food in the dry box behind it. Obviously, we don't do much in the way of fire down belowdecks, but once I get everything chopped and ready I can make a mean pulav on our stove up above. You like pulav?"

Shina's stomach growled at the word, but she just smiled politely and said, "It's all right." She had the feeling that a real heiress would turn her nose up at something that good and that simple.

"We're down to dried fish and lentils right now," said the quartermaster, "but once we get into Jepjep I got a guy who gives me a bleeding deal on fruit and grains."

"That would be nice," Shina said. She wasn't sure if she should offer to add to their eating money. It seemed polite—much too polite for a sugar farmer's daughter among fishermen. "How long do you think we'll be in Jepjep?"

"Oh, I don't know," the quartermaster said. "Long enough to get some good food, maybe a good night's sleep for the Captain. Couple days."

Shina nodded. She kept her face calm, but that was *much* longer than she wanted to stay in port. The temple couldn't be more than a few hours' walk away from the port—and surely Aksa-auntie would understand the urgency of the situation enough to let her leave in a hurry once she had the compass.

"So, let's see," the quartermaster said, walking in a tight circle around the middle of the hold. "Fish crates, sleeping bunks, kitchen—you sure you're all right sharing our accommodations?" She gave her a narrow-eyed half-smile. "It's probably not what you're used to." The smile faded. "At all."

Shina nodded. "I think I'm going to be fine."

"Well, all right." The quartermaster took a deep breath before swinging up onto the rope ladder that took them up from the hold. "Come on up, and I'll show you the oh-shit gear."

· · ·

Topside, Captain Tazir was laughing with her first mate, a bearded mountain of a man with a booming voice and an easy confidence in his walk. Both of them grew silent when they caught sight of Shina. The Captain gave her a polite bow. Shina had no idea if she meant it.

"I hope you find the accommodations to your liking," the Captain said. "We're ready to go north any time you like."

"The sooner the better." Shina tried to mask her nervousness with a grin, but the Captain's flat-mouthed, flat-eyed expression did not change.

"Very well," she said. "Shouldn't be more than twenty minutes or so."

Shina felt her face flush as she trudged over to where the quartermaster was waiting to show her the emergency oars and the air bladders, none of which looked sturdy enough to do any good if they were needed. It wasn't like she had the option to be polite back there—manners weren't going to win back the icon, weren't going to give her the compass. They certainly wouldn't un-burn the school and un-raze the city and—

Shina took a deep breath as she willed that darkness out of her mind. *Not now,* she thought. *Not now.*

"Are you all right?" the quartermaster asked, putting a hand on her arm.

Shina jerked away and snarled at her—and then came back to her senses. "Oh!" She blushed. "I'm sorry, I just—I just—" Her mouth hung open, unwilling or unable to form words that matched what she needed to say. "I'm tired," she said.

"I'm not surprised." The quartermaster smiled. "If you're sure you're happy with the bunking arrangement down below, go ahead and take a nap while we get under way."

"Thank you," Shina said. She bowed and went to the hatch that led belowdecks. From her time helping her father manage his little dhow, she knew that the crew needed her out of the way while they got ready to set out for Jepjep.

Quietly, she slipped off her silk shass set. She'd bought it off a harlot in a nice neighborhood, uphill from Humma's docks where the breeze whispered cool on the verandahs and garden benches. She imagined that if she'd actually come from a place like that, she wouldn't be so excited for the chance to cocoon herself in a well-worn hammock hanging in a hot, muggy hold that reeked of old fish. Or maybe she would. It had been two hellish days since she'd last slept.

· · ·

Her body did not let her stay awake for long, but awful dreams kept her from resting. She was running, running across the sand, running until her lungs pounded but getting no closer to the ship as it pulled away. The flames were different—they spread from Sij Point all the way down to the corner of the island where the school was. They were even out on the water.

She ran, but could not reach the boat. She knew they were behind her—not the flames, but *them,* with their axes and hammers and cruel spears. She could feel hot, meaty breath on the back of her neck.

When she turned around, a man stood behind her with his mouth open too wide for his face. His teeth were sticky with gore. He raised his hammer—Shina tried to move, but her limbs were too thick, too heavy, too—

"Hey. Hey-ey-ey!"

Shina burst through the surface of sleep with a ragged shout. "What!"

Someone—a woman—the quartermaster of the *Giggling Goat* was gripping her shoulder. It was dark. She was fine. She took a sharp, deep breath.

"You were screaming," she whispered. "It's two in the morning."

Shina panted in the dark for a few moments. Her heart was thumping in her chest like a caged animal. "I need to get topside," she muttered, rolling out of the hammock and onto the floor. She was going to start sobbing again. She could *not* afford to start sobbing again.

It was better when she was out of the hold. She lay on the deck, naked save for the short skirt she wore beneath the shass set, and let the breeze run up her body from her toes to the top of her head. She relaxed into it, let her mind trace the currents and soft spots in the air around her. It was a north wind, coaxed into existence weeks ago by the beautiful Tu'ua sisters down in Chut and guided past Humma by Vindi-uncle. It had that rough, sour edge that all the winds had shown since the icon had been stolen—but this was gentle, a shy breeze designed to swirl back into a calm rather than puff up into a storm. It needed no Windspeakers to control it, and this one might last for a week or two before dying on its own.

Shina breathed it in, breathed it out, made that love and that serenity a part of her as best she could. There was sadness in that wind, too. It ran deep and cold, but it was—it was different, somehow, much calmer than the raw grief that had been tearing at her chest only a few minutes ago. Older, maybe, or maybe just more detached from the carnage at Tash.

As her heartbeat slowed down, closer to a meditation rhythm, she started to realize the strange silence at the edge of the breeze. Usually, you could hear whispers where one Windspeaker's work ran into another's—but not tonight. Tonight, perhaps, the Windspeakers were in mourning. Or, perhaps they weren't, and things were worse than Shina thought.

• • •

As the *Giggling Goat* sailed closer to Jepjep, the Captain seemed determined to ignore Shina. She greeted her seldom, and then only with grunts. Shina wondered whether it was genuine dislike, or whether the Captain was just trying to keep a safe distance between herself and a passenger who could be anybody under the sun. In any case, Shina decided she ought to deal with the situation by staying out of everybody's way—especially the first mate's. He had the same black skin, broad nose, and lilting accent that marked Shina and her kin as coming from Mayun. The more time she spent around him, the more she worried that he'd recognize the family tattoos on her right arm or the way she said "weather." It might not turn out to be a big deal, or he might remember the skinny kid from Dos Mejara who made clouds form over puddles in the road.

The second possibility would not be good for Shina. There was a reason that frightened parents put their children on midnight boats to Tash when they turned out to be Windspeakers. There was a reason they were hidden from the world until made safe by surgery. There was a reason the ancient Windspeakers had begged Herself for the icon. A Windspeaker with her powers unchecked caused mayhem, and folks were *intent* on making every wet-eyes Windspeaker pay the full price for it.

Shina slept topside the next night, wrapped in a blanket that the quartermaster had brought up from belowdecks. This time, the dream began with a familiar scene: she was on the operating table, going into deep meditation while the novices swung their opium censers around her face. Matha-auntie and Sura-auntie stood to the side, scrubbing their hands. Somehow, Shina could see it all—could see Hasin-uncle coming down the hallway in the procession of assistants, bearing her new eyes on one silken pillow and the surgery tools on another.

She could hear the noise outside, too. She could hear the shouts of the raiders from the Dragon Ships. She could hear the screams of the students as they were cut down, hear them begging for mercy, even if only for the little children. She could hear the howls, the *laughter,* the sound of breaking glass, of metal being dragged across rock—and still, the operation was proceeding.

Shina tried to rouse herself from her trance, tried to bring conscious thought streaming back into her mind like daylight through a window. *Wake up!* she screamed to herself. The noise outside grew louder. The assistants surrounded her motionless body; Hasin-uncle arranged the eyes and tools around her head.

He opened his mouth, as he always did in these dreams, to direct Sura-auntie to make the first cut—but instead of words, blood poured from his mouth. Shina was trapped in her body again, locked in her trance but still able to look up and see the surgeons, Hasin-uncle, all the young assistants as they had fallen. Monat with his face cleaved in half. Jeppa, her throat cut, trying frantically to form words with her bloody lips.

The last one, she was saying. *You're the last one.*

Those words repeated from every mouth, even Tiga, who was missing the top half of her head when Shina found her. *You're the last one,* they said. *You're the last one. You're the—*

"What is *wrong* with you?" The Captain was shaking her by the shoulders. "Wake up!"

"Ahh!" Shina blinked, shook her head. "Oh, no—oh—what?"

"You were screaming again," the Captain said. "You

kept telling us, 'They're coming, they're coming,' and I been trying to wake you up for damn near a minute."

Shina realized her chest was heaving. "I was having a nightmare," she said.

"I'll say." The Captain stood up and looked at her with the corners of her mouth turned down. "Take some rum—it'll quiet you down some."

"I—I don't drink," said Shina.

The Captain clicked her tongue. "Well, I don't know your life," she said, "but that might be part of your greater overall problem."

While she went back to her patrol of the deck, Shina wrapped the blanket around her shoulder and sat on a fish crate to watch the stars go by. It was almost dawn, and unless she was mistaken, she could see some of the lights of Jepjep on the horizon.

Now and then, the Captain would look Shina over with her eyes narrowed. A few times, she tilted her head and opened her mouth as if to say something, but she stayed silent.

It wasn't until they passed the first jetty that the Captain rubbed the back of her neck and let out a long, acid hiss. The sun was coming up, and the clouds blushed coral violet.

"Well," the Captain said, "we're here." She waved her arm in a broad sweep against the crescent of wooden buildings that lined the docks. "Is it everything you imagined?"

Truth be told, Shina hadn't put much thought into imagining what Jepjep would be like. In her mind, all ports were built on a pile of rocks, just down the beach from a sleepy little straw-roofed village. Humma, with its rows of wooden houses and storehouses and shops all in together with each other, had surprised her with its hustle and bustle. Jepjep, as she had expected, did the same.

Jepjep was built on the southern tip of Moliki, which was first in a little string of eastern-ish islands that boasted snow-capped peaks. The hills started to rear up almost at the water's edge—the city was built on one that was shallower than most. Brightly painted wooden houses grew fancier and fancier as they got higher off the water, and then there was a band of green around a small hut that had to be the storm temple.

"Better put those silks back on," said the Captain, snorting at Shina's openmouthed silence. "You'll find a cleaner bed at an inn if you look nicer."

"Are we staying overnight, then?" Shina raised her brows.

The Captain looked at her with wide eyes and a flat mouth. "You wanna get gone in a hurry, don't you?"

Shina looked at the ground.

"Well, what do you want here?" She clicked her

tongue. "New clothes, I bet—get your hair changed."

"I just need to visit my sister," Shina blurted. "She—she won't be able to help me, but I need to *see* her, all right?"

"Fine." The Captain put her hands up and backed away. "As long as you keep the money coming, my ship is yours."

They didn't speak to each other as the Captain moored the ship to the dock at its east end; when the first mate came up to help her, he communicated only in grunts. They were one of only a few boats tying up in Jepjep that morning. The threat of the Dragon Ships had been keeping boats away from ports like this one, where there was no Prefect rich enough to keep a private navy. Storm temples all around the islands had learned a cruel lesson in how powerless they were against the raiders. Once their natural eyes were replaced with windstones, they lost the ability to create the kind of freakish weather that could destroy ships and ruin towns. They could only aid the Prefects' warriors—and the Prefects didn't have enough swords to guard ports *and* temples.

"I won't be long," Shina said to the Captain as she put her shass set back on. You could tell she'd stowed it, but it wasn't too much the worse for being hung up down below.

"Good," said the Captain. "You can help us get the

supplies loaded."

Shina decided not to ponder whether that was meant as an insult. She trudged down the gangplank and headed along the dock, only stumbling a little bit on legs that were used to a ship's deck.

The sun was climbing, and the streets were waking up. Shopkeepers' children were setting baskets of colorful fruits in front of stores; goats and chickens demanded their morning meals beside the butcher shops. In front of a temple to Shula, a line was forming for public breakfast. Although Shina stopped to bow to the green-haired goddess, she kept a quick pace as she made her way uphill.

Doubts and worries had begun to swarm around her head like flies. She'd only met Aksa-auntie once, and that had been a brief introduction at a temple dedication ceremony. There was no guarantee—maybe not even a likelihood—that she would recognize Shina, that she would recognize Shina as a student Windspeaker, that she would believe that Shina was the last one alive after the raid on Tash.

As she got closer and closer to the temple, Shina became more and more certain that she was in the wrong place. She was passing big, ornate houses now, and servants gave her suspicious glares as they swept the verandahs and hung the shade mats in the eastern openings. The packed sand of the road was becoming rockier and loamier—after it passed a tall purple house with a lush garden in front, it narrowed to a dirt path just wide enough for a pushcart.

Just approaching the temple was enough to calm Shina's thumping heart a little bit. No, it wasn't the temple on Tash, or one of the familiar rural temples where the students would go to learn alongside the grown Windspeakers, but it was a storm temple nonetheless. Wherever Shina went, these simple round mud huts with their roofs of dried leaves would be home.

When she reached the threshold of the hut, Shina knelt and prostrated herself. After a few moments, she heard an old woman clear her throat.

"You can come in," said a worn voice. Shina rose, tightened the bottom knot on her shass, and stepped inside the temple.

Aksa-auntie sat, as was customary for Windspeakers, on a round seat of black stone that had been brought up from the Sunrise Temple on Vihar. Dressed only in a simple linen frock, she had her white curls shorn as short as Shina's. She had always been a small woman, and in her old age her posture had become stooped from the weight of her eyes. Although the heavy stone orbs had been pitch black when they'd been put in (like everyone else's), nearly seventy years in Aksa-auntie's head had turned them a beautiful pale pink. The green veins spreading across them had begun to develop purple spots like flowers on a vine.

"You're nervous," Aksa-auntie said, cocking her ears toward Shina. Her button nose twitched as she sniffed the air. "You smell like smoke, and you've been on a fishing boat." Aksa-auntie beckoned for Shina to come over. She grasped in the air as she approached. When Shina was close enough, Aksa-auntie grabbed her skirt and held it to her nose, then gripped her leg and felt her way up to her hand. Shina winced at the touch, but let Aksa-auntie pull her arm to her face and sniff it.

"You're wearing clothes that aren't yours," she said. She sat back, took a deep breath, and let out a short laugh. "And you hurried up here."

"Yes, auntie," Shina said.

"Give me your face."

Shina held her breath and shut her eyes as she bent down for Aksa-auntie's inspection. The old woman's thin, frail hands were gentle as they brushed against her cheeks, prodded at her eyelids to see if they contained living flesh or cold stone.

"You know," Aksa-auntie said as she released Shina's head, "I once told somebody that I hoped I'd never give this compass to anybody." She motioned for Shina to step back and stood up, leaning on a rough wooden staff. "But now that you're here—" She shook her head as she walked to a patch of the reed mat floor and started thumping her stick against it. When it rang hollow, she knelt and picked up a section of the mat. Under the mat was a board, and under the board was a hole. Inside the hole was a sealed jar, which Aksa-auntie lifted with a smile.

"Here it is, my dear," she said, holding it toward Shina. A wry smile crawled across her round, wizened face as she rattled it. "Go on—give the jar a good smash. Make it count."

Shina took the jar in both hands. She stared at it, surprised by its weight and aghast that Aksa-auntie was so—so *irreverent* about it. "Smash it?" she said. "Are you—"

"You'll only get to do this once in a lifetime." The old Windspeaker held up a finger. "If I were you, I'd take the chance to make some noise."

Shina swallowed and raised the jar above her head. "Here goes," she said.

She brought the jar down with all the might in her arms. When it hit the floor, there was no crash of breaking pottery, but instead, a clap of thunder that made Shina jump and made Aksa-auntie throw her head back and roar with laughter.

"That's the spirit!" the Windspeaker said, waving her walking stick in the air.

Shina gasped as the shards of the pot shuddered, burst into flame, and dissolved into black smoke. When the smoke took the shape of five black birds and began circling her head, she squealed.

"Now open your mouth!" cackled the Windspeaker.

She didn't have to tell Shina to do that—her mouth was already gaping—but she could have warned Shina that she might choke and cough as the birds flew down her throat one by one. She sank to her knees, trying not to vomit in this sacred place as she hacked and coughed.

The Windspeaker was giggling now, circling Shina at an excited hobble.

"Oh, yes, oh, yes," she was saying. "It's you, all right. It all depends on you."

On the floor by her hand, Shina noticed a stone ball she hadn't seen before. It was pure milky white—except, when Shina picked it up, a red spot appeared on its surface. No matter which way she turned the stone, the dot stayed in the same place, just at the edge of the top right quadrant.

"Those storms will not come out of you any easier than they went in," said Aksa-auntie. "And if you ask me, they're likely to be much worse."

"Storms?" Shina grimaced. "Entire storms?" Releasing a storm could kill you if you still had your wet eyes. "But—but how do I—"

"Don't ask me," Aksa-auntie said as she walked back to her chair. "Until you bring the icon back, the only things I know about Windspeaking are the ones that come from here—" She touched her ear. "And here—" She tapped her nose. "So I would hurry, if I were you." She settled herself back on her seat with her walking stick in her lap.

"Is—is this—all?" Shina asked, cocking her head to one side.

Aksa-auntie shrugged. "I'm afraid that your teachers were being very literal when they told you that we're powerless without the icon in its proper place." She shook her head. "Don't want a bunch of useless old ladies with big mouths? Find it. Bring it home." She smiled up at Shina. "We trust you."

Shina nodded. "Thank you, auntie," she said.

"Don't thank me," the Windspeaker replied, picking up her stick and waving it. "Get out and bring us our power back!"

Chapter 3

Tazir cracked one eye open, then shut it again. She drew her knees to her chest and sucked in a slow, deep breath. She was getting too old to drink like this.

"Fuck," she groaned, rubbing her temples with her fingertips.

"Ehhhn?" Chaqal's warm, soft form shifted in the hammock beside hers. She put a hand on Tazir's shoulder.

"*Fuck!*" Tazir repeated.

"Nnhhhn." Chaqal shifted again. "I'm getting too old to drink like this," she groaned.

"Don't even start." Tazir brushed Chaqal's hand aside, sat up, and waited for her head to stop swimming. "I—" The rest of the sentence had already left her brain. "Hmm." She smacked her lips together for a few moments. Something was wrong. Out of place. Off schedule—

"Oh, what the *hell*," Tazir growled as she swung over and put her feet on the floor. "Broad damn daylight, and you don't wake me up for the morning shift."

Chaqal reached out and grasped her wrist. "The kid's doing the deck," she murmured. "Remember?"

"What?" Tazir turned around to glare down at her quartermaster.

"I told you," Chaqal said. "She came by this morning." She was beautiful like this, squinting up at Tazir with her hair flying around her face. Black tattoos spiraled down her arms, turning into fish here and leaves there. She'd had some already when she'd met Tazir. Most of them were newer.

"Come back to bed," Chaqal said.

"You just took that girl at her word?"

"Kodin was with her." She tugged gently at Tazir's wrist. "Come on—the fruit place isn't even open yet."

Tazir yanked her hand away and pulled her chest bindings from where she hung them above the hammock. She hissed all the air out of her lungs while she wound the dirty linen around her heavy breasts. As she bent over to tie the knot behind her back, she heard Chaqal groan.

"For the love of—" she said. "Why do you have to be like this?"

"I'll tell you why!" Tazir snapped. "Because I *own* this ship and I *care* about this ship and I don't want—"

"I *said* Kodin was with her," said Chaqal. She sat up, rubbing her eyes. "Come on, Cap. I just wanted to give you a morning off."

"You don't give me *shit*," Tazir said, putting her vest on over the wraps and storming over to the hatchway. "It ain't your place."

• • •

She regretted those words as she patrolled the deck, her arms crossed and her pipe clamped between her lips. It had always stung like hell when Mati used to tell her what was and wasn't her place—but then again, Chaqal wasn't her wife, and Mati hadn't been the Captain of the ship.

"That's why you don't shit where you eat, I guess," Tazir muttered to herself, staring out at the blank sea. They had a good wind—a *great* wind, actually—that was moving them northeast at the same no-nonsense pace they'd made all day yesterday. Maybe the Windspeakers had finally stopped mourning Tash and gotten to work.

As she paced, she couldn't help but glance at Shina sleeping on the mat she'd set out on the deck. She was a great deal quieter when she was in the open air. Tazir figured that whatever nightmare-giving horror happened to her must have happened indoors.

"You still don't believe me," Kodin said. It was her fifth or sixth lap around the ship, and far from the first time he'd caught her glancing at Shina.

"I believe that you *want* me to believe you." Tazir glared at the boards below her feet. The salt, scum, and moss that tended to accumulate on ships' decks had indeed been scrubbed off with stones already. Tazir hadn't been able to find a square inch that hadn't been done to her standards. "I guess I'd believe that she told you where you missed a spot."

"It's not that hard to scrub a deck," Kodin said. "You know she likes being helpful."

Tazir looked at the great length of girl curled up on the mat, her smooth skin rippled by her backbone and the gentle contours of ribs. She was snoring gently—a vast improvement over the moaning and yelling.

"Probably can't sleep until she wears herself out," Tazir said. "It's good for these rich kids." Despite her best intentions, poking fun at Shina had lost some of its fun.

Kodin shook his head and flattened his mouth. "I don't know what happened to her," he said, "but I doubt it was good."

"Yeah?" Tazir shrugged. "Well, it was good for us."

"Don't say that." He sank his brows over his eyes. "She's just a kid."

Tazir took a long pull on her pipe. "I guess," she grumbled, squinting into the sun. There was no sign of the island they were supposed to be passing by the afternoon. "Where were we at dawn?" she asked.

"Just leaving Mun behind," he said.

Tazir snorted so hard, she nearly blew her tobacco out into the water. "What?"

"The wind kept up all night," said Kodin. "Hope we didn't stumble into someone's private merchant route, but I haven't seen any ships yet."

Tazir laughed. "You can't bribe a Windspeaker to make a wind run this long," she said. "Their high temple or whatever won't let them."

"You never know," he said, crossing his arms. "Wet-eyes aren't common, but they happen."

"Mm-hmm." Tazir rolled her eyes and smiled. Kodin had been raised just south of the temple on Tash, where they taught young Windspeakers to control their abilities. Sometimes, full-grown Stormcallers with wet eyes and dangerous talents were brought to the school in chains, to have those eyes gouged out and replaced with stones that reined them in. Some of the stories that came with those rogues were enough to entertain even a grizzled sailor like Tazir.

"Sometimes," Kodin murmured, "they show up in pickup bars in blouses that don't fit them right."

"Uh-huh," Tazir said. She took a long draw on her pipe. "So you're telling me that some twenty-year-old wet-eyes, who can spit storms well enough that she can sing up a wind like this"—she pointed at the red-and-purple-striped sail of the *Giggling Goat*—"has to drop forty thousand qyda on some pisstub fishing boat to take her up to the long banks for no reason."

Kodin frowned. "She has the Tashi accent," he said. "The Dragon Ships hit that temple hard—burned them all alive, I heard."

"You been letting pretty Myrans blow smoke at you again," Tazir said.

"Nah, these were Tashi." Kodin arched his heavy brows. "Said they tortured the nurses until they told them where they were hiding the children."

"I guess that's a step up from describing the pretty virgins they were raping," Tazir snorted. "They're just thieves, Kodin. They show up at places with bad security, they take what they can as fast as they can, and they leave enough wreckage behind them to get away."

"We've seen gangs of thieves before," Kodin said. "Those ships are full of monsters."

"You know," Tazir said, "I've found that the biggest difference between a common crook and a—a superhuman abomination is usually a few degrees of being good at your job."

"See, this is why I won't go through the Tejji Mists with you." He shook his head. "Everybody's gotta be just as beady-eyed and practical as you are—"

"Oh, I'm beady-eyed now?"

"Beady-eyed and salt-knuckled." Kodin rolled his eyes. "You'd sell the wind itself—"

"I would do *exactly* that." Tazir smiled. "None of this 'I'm gonna make it rain on my island and fuck up the winds for two months' amateur chickenshit—that's how the school catches them, you know." She puffed on her pipe. "Nah, if that were me, I'd be real quiet about it. Maybe practice a little bit here and there, get just good enough to kick up a little wind."

"I know a few stories that start just like that," Kodin snorted. "They can't control the power they have—not forever."

"Oh, sure, that's what they *say*," said Tazir. "How the fuck else are you going to get a kid to live in a monastery for a decade and then get his eyes gouged out? What the fuck kind of life is that?"

"They got some religious thing going on," Kodin said.

"Yeah, they *religiously* tell the kid he's a monster and beat him down into accepting his lot in life like a damn dairy goat." Tazir puffed on her pipe and shook her head. "I bet there's some wet-eye Windspeakers out there who are clever enough not to get hauled to that slaughter-house in chains." She took the pipe out of her mouth and pointed it at Kodin. "But if they're that clever, then they're probably making a hell of a lot of money some-where else." She put the pipe back in her mouth. "Besides, if she's got the Tash accent, what's she even doing with those eyeballs? More likely she killed a servant by accident and needs to hide out for a while."

"Maybe," Kodin said. "I'm just saying, that wind didn't drop a lick all last night, and it's skidding us right up—"

They both turned around at the sound of a drawn-out grunt behind them. The kid thrashed her legs, muttering something into the blanket that covered her face. She went quiet, curled up, and then let out a sigh.

"You awake?" Tazir asked.

Shina was silent for a moment, then curled tighter, then stretched out slowly and groaned. For the first time, Tazir noticed the soles of her feet—worn down and hardened by a long time walking with no shoes.

"Yeah," Shina said, sitting up. She raised her arms over her head and rolled her neck around. A great yawn filled her lanky form, thrashed it around on its way out. "What time is it?" she asked.

"On about nine hours," Tazir said. She took a step back, looking the kid up and down. "Kodin here says you been scrubbing the deck with him."

Shina nodded, covering this yawn with one hand. "I was awake," she said. "Might as well help."

"Hmph." Tazir nodded. Nervously, she cracked a smile at Shina. "Thanks, then."

"You're welcome." Shina smiled back, blinking into the sun.

• • •

By the time Tazir climbed back down into the hold, Chaqal had already set breakfast. The table was folded out and secured with its straps. A big bowl of doli, two bladders of water, and a basket of sliced fruit were all wobbling back and forth within its raised border. The quartermaster herself was relaxing in her hammock, her own skin of water in one hand and papaya on her face.

"Everything all right up there?" she asked.

"Yeah," Tazir said. "The kid helped Kodin do the deck, I guess."

"You *guess*?"

"I don't fuckin'—" Tazir picked up a bladder and took a few big gulps of water. "Just, let's not talk about the kid, all right?"

"All right," Chaqal said. Her thick, long brows were arched in a semicircle on her forehead. "No need to ask how the rum's treating you."

"Sorry." Tazir shut her eyes and took in a deep breath. "It's just—she's making me nervous, you know?"

Chaqal grunted as she got out of the hammock. She was dressed again in her plain, dumpy working clothes.

"Nervous?" she asked.

"You seen her feet?" Tazir pointed at her with the doli spoon.

Chaqal shook her head. "You know, I'm not really a foot girl."

Tazir rolled her eyes. "You know what I'm saying," she said. "I saw her up there this morning—she looks like she's never owned a pair of shoes in her life."

"And that makes you nervous because . . ." Chaqal blinked at her.

"It doesn't strike you as strange at all that a girl who's never owned shoes is blowing forty thousand qyda on a trip to the long banks in a fifty-foot dhow?" Tazir raised her eyebrows and took another gulp of water from the bladder.

"Not if she stole more than forty thousand qyda," said Chaqal.

Tazir was struck by the sudden need to defend the kid from this brazen accusation. "How the hell do you steal forty thousand qyda?"

"I don't know," she said. "That's why I work on a fishing boat and don't ask questions when people want to *give me* forty thousand qyda!"

Tazir grunted and started shoveling doli into her mouth. Now that they could afford to put some lemon juice and chili pepper in it, the root mash was almost delicious. As she ate, Kodin came down the hatch and started fixing his own meal of doli and fruit.

"Shina spotted land," he said.

Chaqal choked on her water and coughed. "What?"

"We've had a weird wind," Kodin went on. "Think we're in somebody's payoff route."

"All right," Chaqal said. "And the mysterious rich person with the Tash accent isn't—you know—" She narrowed her eyes and made a wiggly motion with one hand. "We're not suspecting her of maybe—"

"The Captain won't hear of it," Kodin said. "And she's awake now, so watch it."

"Fine by me," Chaqal said. She set her jaw and gave Tazir a wide-eyed stare. "But don't tell us we didn't warn you."

Tazir glared up at Chaqal's ass as she climbed abovedecks.

"You know I'm right," Kodin said through a bite of guava.

Tazir sucked down some more water and shook her head. "You read into things too much," she said. "Why would we care if you're right?"

"Guess I don't have an answer for that one," Kodin said. He gulped down his bowl of doli, set his bowl down, and got settled into the farthest hammock from the table.

• • •

They arrived in Kuhon around six in the evening—a full day and a half ahead of what Tazir would have called "good time." Tazir watched Shina carefully as she helped Chaqal and Kodin into the slip. Kuhon didn't have a dock that served boats this small, but when the tide was high, you could pull up all the way into a sandy slip marked by log pontoons.

At least one of them had been keeping a wary eye on Shina all day. If not Tazir, then it had been Chaqal or Kodin. They weren't obvious about it—one nice thing about sailing a fifty-foot dhow was that it made it easy to watch someone discreetly. Nonetheless, all those hours of observation failed to yield any new information about Shina. She was awkward, soft-spoken, and eager to do anything that might get a smile or an approving nod from someone on the ship. But Shina didn't work like Mati had, cautiously, in stops and starts. She watched patiently as the crew showed her the basics of a task, and she did it as quickly and easily as if she'd been doing it her whole life.

"We're early," Tazir remarked to her. The more she watched the kid, the weirder she felt speaking to her in grunts and single words. She elaborated: "We're *really* fuckin' early."

"Are we?" Shina asked. "That's good, though."

"I guess." Tazir took in a deep breath. "I'd say we'll have time to sleep in real beds tonight."

Shina looked at her but said nothing. One corner of her mouth turned down.

"What?"

The kid opened her mouth, but then looked out to the beach again. "How do we get off the ship?" she asked.

"We jump," Tazir said. "Just one more reason I'm keen to find somewhere I can get a bed and find a laundry."

Shina sucked in a deep, slow breath. Her jaw tightened, but she made no other move. "Well," she said, "if that's the case, I guess I'd better put my clothes in a bag."

• • •

For once, Tazir took her chance to put on port clothes that were a little nicer than the ones she'd left in a sopping pile at the inn. She wasn't a shass set girl, but she could cut a fine figure in a pair of black silk trousers and a kidskin vest.

"Come on," she was saying as she pushed a mug of rum and lime toward the kid. "Everybody *drinks*." They had managed to get into a nice corner table at Bosso's.

It was a decent little rum joint on the second tier of the port, held up from the beach on long bamboo legs and walled with reed mats. A plump barmaid with her hair up in a red scarf patrolled the tables, and a pair of young men with shaven heads played quiet water drums in the corner.

"I just—I just don't like it," Shina said. "I don't like the way it tastes, and—"

"You've been drinking goat piss liquor," Tazir assured her. "Just try it."

"Come on, Cap," Chaqal said, laying a hand on her arm. "Leave her be."

Shina smiled at Chaqal over the rim of her teacup.

Tazir rolled her eyes and took a good long swig of her own drink. "Have you ever had a day of fun in your life?" she asked, leaning back in her chair. "Or is it all—whatever you did on that sugar farm of yours that wasn't drinking or wearing shoes?"

Shina's eyebrows popped up; she choked on her tea for a moment behind a balled-up hand. "I—I don't—"

"Captain!" Chaqal hissed through gritted teeth.

"It doesn't matter to *me* where you're from," Tazir said. "Just doesn't seem from looking at you that it was the best place in the world."

Shina's mouth hung open for a moment; her teacup hovered in mid-drink. "I—I was happy where I came from," she said. She blinked, looking Tazir in the eye. "And I'm happy where I am now."

"I don't believe that for a moment."

"Captain!"

Tazir hissed and rounded on Chaqal. "Dammit, woman," she growled. "Would you keep—hey!" she yelled fruitlessly at a big man in heavy braids who'd bumped into her on his way out of the bar. He wasn't the only one. Patrons were fleeing the bar like hens from a busted cage.

The kid had put her teacup down. She was staring into her lap with a weird, scared grimace on her face. She stood up, reached across the table, and clasped Tazir's arm. "They're here," she said. Her other hand was thrust deep in her skirt pocket. "They're *here*—come on!"

It took a moment for Tazir to pick up what the kid meant by *they*, but when she did she dropped her drink. "Oh, *fuck*," she said, searching the crowd for Kodin. She spotted the top of his head above the crowd, over by the bar.

"Come on!" said the kid.

Tazir yanked her arm away and shoved forward. "Not without my first mate!"

Chapter 4

Shina's heart raced in her chest as Tazir disappeared into the mob of drunken sailors. "Captain?" she called after her. A pair of old women nearly bowled her over as they fled, but Chaqal steadied her on her feet.

"She'll be out in a minute," said the quartermaster. "Come on—this is gonna get *ugly*."

The air in the bar crackled with fear and confusion. The barman was putting the liquor away; people yelled at him to keep serving. Shina let Chaqal lead her by the wrist, her free hand stuffed in her skirt pocket and curled tight around her compass.

Inside her stomach, Shina could feel her four remaining storms growing restless. The next one she spat out, she knew, would not be as easy on her as the breeze that had carried them from Jepjep.

The Dragon Ships are here, she thought. The crowd in the bar surged and billowed, a strange wave she could neither understand nor control. *And they don't believe it yet.*

"Captain!" Shina called again over her shoulder. They

were outside the bar now. If worst came to worst, she could dive off the dock and swim back to the *Giggling Goat.* "Captain, you have to—"

"Follow us!" Tazir came barreling out of the rush of people, Kodin on her tail. She pointed down the dock, toward the slip where they'd moored the vessel. Shina followed the three of them as they sprinted south. They were not alone. Men and women—and now, more and more children—were fleeing the city. Shina did not dare look behind her. The compass was growing hot in her grip.

It didn't take them long to reach the end of the dock. When they did, the Captain didn't keep going toward the ship—instead she veered left, followed some of the people from the bar toward the heavy green wall of jungle at the top of the sand.

"Where are you going?" Shina called. "What—"

"We're getting the hell away from the harbor!" Tazir snapped. "The boat's an easy target!"

"No!" Shina yelled. "No, you can't!" She couldn't keep this pace up much longer. "We have to get back to the ship!"

"Not today we don't!" Kodin yelled. "Hurry up!"

"Come back!" Shina yelled. She was standing stock-still in the sand, her fists balled at her sides. The compass had grown so hot, it burned her hand.

"Look, sweetie," the quartermaster said, hurrying over to Shina, "I know you want to get north, and I know you have a *fuck ton* of money, but—"

"Hold up." The Captain stepped toward them. "You mind explaining to us *why* you want us to go back to the boat right now?"

"I can't," she blurted. Not here, not pressed for time like this, and certainly not while trying to hold in this storm. "I—I can't."

"What do you mean, you *can't*?" Tazir barked. "You've got a mouth in your head, don't you?"

"It's—just believe me, all right?" Her belly churned and ached. To distract herself, she ran her thumb in a painful circle around the compass. "I can get us out of here, but we have to get to the boat."

"I don't know where you think we're from," said the Captain, "but it ain't a place where we're just gonna take your word on it and sit in a boat while these sons of bitches burn the town down around us."

"Let's go!" Kodin said. "Whatever plan you have, ours is better."

"I have to get back to the ship," Shina pleaded. She couldn't hold the storm in much longer—and when it came out, it was going to be awfully hard to explain herself to these frantic islanders running from the approaching raiders. "Look!" She pulled her hand from her pocket and held the compass aloft. It was glowing now, a bright sunset pink that stood out against the darkening sky.

The Captain hissed and drew back as if she'd touched it herself, her eyes wide and her teeth bared. "What the fuck is that?"

"It's a compass," Shina said. "Sort of."

"Did it tell you the Dragon Ships were coming?" said the Captain.

"Yes!" Shina said. "I can—I can explain everything, I promise, but I need to be back at the ship." A breeze—a product not of the storm in Shina's gut, but of the nervousness pounding through her veins—was starting to whip across the beach. It wouldn't be long now.

Kodin stepped toward her. "And why in the hell can't you—"

Without a word, Shina turned and sprinted back toward the boat. The breeze was picking up, chilling the beach and speeding her feet. She could see them, now—two of the great longboats pulling around the northern tip of Kuhon.

"Hey, wait!" Chaqal called after her. "Ohhhhhhhh, if you wreck our boat—"

As she got closer to the water, it was easier for Shina to run. She hadn't been planning on piloting a fifty-foot dhow by herself. She didn't even know if she could. It certainly wasn't something that people did because they wanted to.

"Dammit, girl," came a voice from behind her. Was it the Captain's? Shina was wading toward the boat's ladder; her head was spinning. She clutched at the compass. She couldn't lose the compass—she couldn't fall into the water—but it was so hard to stand—

Shina reached out to balance on something before she fell, but there was nothing there. She splashed and flailed in the water, dimly aware that the storm was escaping from her gut but not at all sure of what it was becoming once it got out.

"Holy *shit*—"

"For fuck's sake, don't *drop* her!"

"I'm *trying*—"

"Try harder!"

Shina's rib cage pulsed; her jaws ached as if strange hands were forcing them open.

"What do I do?"

"Here—keep her head down so it don't flow into her lungs—"

"Holy *shit*!"

"Or you can *keep screaming*—"

"You're not helping either. Now, step to the side—good—"

Shina began to cough and spit. She'd shut her eyes against the salt water, and couldn't bear to open them again. Her insides burned like she'd swallowed the—*where was it?*

"My compass," she gasped. "Where is my compass?"

"Fuck—Kodin, do you see it down there?"

"I need my compass—" Shina kept fighting for air. She needed to breathe—why was it so *hard*?

"Okay, hand her up here."

Shina tried to figure out who was hoisting her up on their shoulders—was it Chaqal? The Captain?

"Fuck!" The first mate's voice came from somewhere below her. "This thing's *hot*!"

The Captain grunted as she handed her off; the quartermaster hauled Shina's quaking body over the ship's railing and set her down on the deck.

Before Shina was aware of the faces leaning in over her, she was aware of the storm. It didn't have any real cloud power yet—but that was building. In a way, it was like the storm got louder as it drew in the moisture from the sky around it, sucking the air dry for miles. The wind howled, sending stinging sand across the deck of the *Giggling Goat* and tugging at its sails.

"Get out," Shina croaked at the looming faces. "Get out of the harbor."

"We can't," Kodin said. "The tide isn't in yet."

"Push the boat out," Shina said. She let her eyes drift shut, let her mind drift out along the water with that whipping wind. It was running high and strong and heavy with moisture. She let her breath merge with the wind, found places where she could part it and twist it, grab hold of it with her brain and nudge its course a little bit one way or another.

"Put the sail out, too," said her mouth, somewhere else.

There were voices over her body, she could tell. People who'd never seen someone call a storm before. Something stung part of her—her hand, she recalled. Something was burning her hand.

When the sail of the *Giggling Goat* flapped open, it came as a hiccup in the very bottom of a wind. Shina focused on the boat, focused on stroking it gently with the wind, making a little almond-shaped eddy where the wind blew firmly and helpfully instead of wanton and wild.

Somewhere far away, she felt something else—kind of a burning like the one on her hand, but more like an emotion than a physical sense. As she tried to figure out what it was, it grew more intense, more discernible. She still couldn't identify it, but she was certain of two things.

First, that second point of burning light was with the Dragon Ships at the north end of the harbor.

Second, she had to get closer to it.

Shina turned her attention back to the water that

lapped around the keel of the boat. That alone wasn't going to push it out into the harbor—but if she could create a storm surge, she might manage it.

And then what are you going to do? said a nagging voice in her head. *Fight off all those men by yourself? Plunder the hold?* Those ships were wide and shallow, she could tell, with holds fat and hollow as clay jugs—it was in the way they thrummed against the wind. Against the wind—

She forced the words "Stay on the boat" out of her mouth, but she had no idea if anyone was there to hear them. Her thoughts were spread out over close to a square mile of ocean, and she had important work to do. That storm surge didn't just need to be high enough to float the *Giggling Goat;* it had to drown the Dragon Ships while it was at it.

It was pointless to try to move too much of a storm at the same time. You had to work in little filaments, no bigger than the breeze that Shina had hissed out of her belly one day at a time to get them this far. It was hard work; she could barely focus when that point of burning pain was drawing so much of her attention.

If you had patience, though, then working slow was rewarding. Slowly but surely, howling all the way, the wind would twist in your grip and go where you wanted it to go.

Shina angled a sharp, water-moving breeze around

until it was facing the eddy where the *Giggling Goat* lay. She realized she was groaning with effort as she pushed the wind in and down, in and down, in and—

"Hold fast!" the Captain yelled, somewhere far away. Shina felt something jerking on her body as the water rushed onto the beach. She slammed into the storm surge with every ounce of effort she had in her body—it was enough to send her into the warm, deep darkness that waited for her on the other side of a storm.

"Get the compass!" was the last thing she heard.

• • •

When Shina came to, the quartermaster was leaning over her. She had one hand on her cheek, the other clasping a leather pouch.

"Can you see me all right?" she asked.

Shina went to answer, but her voice cracked in her throat. She swallowed, coughed. "Yeah," she said. "Did we make it out?"

"Yeah," said Chaqal. "Did *you* do that?"

"I had to," Shina said. Her face flushed—she felt as if a teacher had caught her bending winds without permission. "I—I have to stop those ships." She flailed her arms for a moment, brought herself back to a sitting position.

"I'm not so sure about trying right now," Chaqal said.

"Oh, hold up—"

Shina was getting to her feet, wobbling and tripping all over herself. Her shass set was soaked and clinging to her skin; something had scraped her arm badly during the storm.

"I've got you," Chaqal said, taking her by the arm that wasn't injured. She steadied Shina and walked her to the rail of the ship.

They were about a hundred yards from the shore—Tazir and Kodin were scrambling with the strong wind, desperate to keep the boat off the harbor's bottom. The south beach was thick with panicking villagers. They ran for their lives with their little ones and possessions bundled on their backs.

Shina's eyes were reluctant to turn northward, but she made herself look anyway. The Dragon Ships were just about to reach the shore. Although the storm might have slowed them a little bit, it had not blown them out to sea. When they'd furled their square sails, their ships had three banks of oars to power them along.

A shriek of metal on metal came from the northern end of the harbor. A group of huts was consumed immediately in a fireball that spewed wood and sand and smoke and stone. Shina heard screams of pain join the fearful, desperate wails of Kuhon's people.

"Was that a fucking trebuchet?" yelled the Captain.

"Where in the hell did they get a trebuchet?"

"I have to sink them," Shina said, shutting her eyes. She laid her mind down on the storm as if she were curling up in a blanket; instantly, sleep washed over her.

· · ·

She woke on the deck, Chaqal cradling her head in her hands.

"Hey now," she said, petting Shina's hair. "I told you not to—"

"I have to sink the Dragon Ships!" Shina said.

"Sweetie, you're gonna sink *our* ship if you try to spit a storm in the state you're in." The quartermaster brushed Shina's flailing arm aside and shook her head. "You gotta—"

With a pained grunt, Shina rolled herself over and got onto her knees. Her whole body was shaking; she swayed on all fours like a drunken goat. For a moment, she thought she was going to throw up, but the feeling passed.

The thought kept repeating in her head. She crawled toward the railing, and the quartermaster followed her a couple of steps behind. When she finally got there, she grasped the slick wooden rail and panted while she tried to keep her stomach behind her throat.

The smell of smoke had begun to infect the wind. It filled Shina's nose, and she finally had to shut her eyes and retch over the railing. "I can't," she groaned, clinging to the ship. "Oh, *dammit*, I *can't*—"

"It's okay, sweetie," the quartermaster was saying. She had knelt beside Shina; she was rubbing her lower back and cooing in her ear. "You've done all you can do—the Captain's gonna take us out."

"No, y-you, you don't understand," Shina said. It was getting hard to form words, hard to keep her eyes focused. On the shores of Kuhon, flames were spreading like the wings of horrible birds. "I have to sink them—I have to stop them—"

"We're gonna get away just fine, sweetie," said the quartermaster. "Come on, why don't you relax down below."

A louder scream rose above the rest, and Shina knew that the Dragon Ships had made landfall. She began to squeak and sniffle until she found herself clutching the railing, sobbing into the wind.

"Goddammit, Chaqal," called Tazir from where she was working the sail. "Get her below and get your fat ass up here!"

Shina tried to fight the quartermaster as she was peeled away from the railing, but it was no use. Wrangling the storm had torn every last ounce of strength from her limbs, and she hung limp in the other woman's embrace as they hobbled across the deck to the hatchway.

The quartermaster dropped Shina down the hatch as gently as she could; Shina tried to stand at the bottom, but fell into a heap instead.

"Oh, sweetie, it's all right." Chaqal bent down to scoop Shina up, and realized that she was still sobbing. "Let's just get you into bed here."

"I let it happen," Shina said. "I—I just *stood there* and—"

"Hush, hush." The quartermaster helped her get into a hammock. "It's gonna be fine."

"No, it's not," Shina whimpered. The ship was groaning in the wind; waves beat against its hull. The storm was on its own now. Whoever had built it must have known that it would be much stronger than the one who called it.

"It will," the quartermaster insisted. "We still have the ship, and we still have our lives and limbs." She shuffled in her pocket. "And," she said as she pressed a hot ball of leather into Shina's palm, "we still have this."

Chapter 5

Tazir longed to gulp the water down, to put the skin to her lips and suck it dry in two or three mighty swallows. Instead, she forced herself to take it in sip by conscientious sip. They were two days out from the nearest port, and they had less water than she liked to stock on the average day voyage.

And the kid still hadn't woken up.

"We're picking up a little speed," said Chaqal as she sat down beside her. "The wind's still strong on our fore."

Tazir grunted as she corked her water skin again. If the wind coming in to Kuhon had been freakishly good, then the wind coming out was just as freakishly bad. The whole point of the *Giggling Goat*'s design was that she could trudge through pretty much any wind, but these swirling garbage breezes on the edge of a sudden magic storm—this was, to put it mildly, an interesting challenge.

"Come on," her quartermaster said. "We made it out."

"Yeah?" Tazir fought the urge to spit over the railing behind her. "Lot of good that does us now."

"Look, we'll be in Moliki in two days." Chaqal rolled her eyes and stretched. "And we've stretched water thinner than this before."

"That doesn't mean I like doing it," Tazir grumbled. "Besides, you don't know what's gonna happen between here and there." She swept her arm in the general direction of Moliki. "We could get attacked or becalmed or blown half the way to fuckin' Darjai by the time our wind wakes up again."

"We'll make it fine," Chaqal said. "I think the storm's pissed itself out."

For the last day and a half, they'd had their eyes glued to the south, watching the storm that had begun as weird grey vomit. It billowed high above Kuhon, blocking the sun and whipping the water beneath it into a sheet of grey foam. The *Giggling Goat* was lucky to have escaped before it gathered its full strength—Tazir had weathered some nasty shit, but a black wall of a storm like that was enough to make even the hardest sailor hunker down in a bar somewhere.

Now, the storm had either moved south or grown smaller. It was still lined up right with Kuhon, which was now smoldering in the sunlight. Now and then, Tazir swore she could catch a whiff of wood smoke and charred flesh coming from the port.

"Is she awake?" asked Chaqal.

Tazir shook her head and pulled her pipe from her sash. "Moanin' and cryin' like she's coming off some harsh dope," she said. It was just as annoying as it had been on the way into Kuhon, but really now. What kind of rank sow was gonna complain about a girl, freaky and unnatural and severely misguided or not, who'd pulled that shit to save her?

"I can't say I blame her," Chaqal said. She frowned at the hatchway. "That's—watching that happen—"

"And not for the first time, either." Tazir shook her head and packed a fresh wad of tobacco into the pipe.

Chaqal opened her mouth to say something, then shut it and nodded. "Yeah."

"Yeah, what?" Tazir raised an eyebrow at her as she lit her pipe.

"I was *agreeing* with you, Cap," Chaqal said. "I do that sometimes."

"Hmmph." Tazir took a puff of the sweet tobacco and shook her head. "At least you're being subtle, I guess."

"Subtle about what?"

"You knew she was a runaway wet-eyes this whole time," Tazir said. "So now you get to gloat."

For a few moments, her quartermaster looked at her with her mouth flat and her brows lowered over her eyes. Then, she shook her head and leaned back against the ship's railing. "Sorry, I guess."

"Sorry for what?"

"For whatever I *did*," Chaqal said. "Ever since Shina spat that storm up, you been glaring and muttering and snappin' at me like it's my first week on board."

"Oh, is that all?" Tazir let out a sharp-edged laugh. "Well, excuse *me*," she said, standing up. "Next time I get blown out to sea with a thin-stocked larder and *no fucking water*, I'll make sure to kiss my quartermaster's ass a little more sweetly." She bowed deeply to Chaqal.

"So you *do* think this is my fault, don't you?" The younger woman rolled her eyes. "It's always got to be *someone's* fault. Bad things just don't *happen* for—"

"Bad things happen every damn day of my life!" Tazir snapped. "But me and Kodin and the kid down there, we're *prepared* when they fucking happen!"

"Oh, so you *like* Shina now?"

"Yeah," Tazir said. "I have a tendency to like people who make themselves fucking *useful*."

With that, she turned around and stormed to the hatchway. Chances were, the kid was still asleep, which at least made her company a far sight better than Chaqal's was right now.

Shina didn't even stir in her hammock when Tazir came thumping down into the hold. She must have worn herself out wailing and thrashing, at least for the time being. For the moment, she was just snoring—maybe get-

78

ting some mumbling in there while she was at it.

Truth be told, Tazir wasn't sure what to do with Shina when she was like this. She'd never had any babies of her own, and for good reason—mothering came as naturally to her as goat herding came to an eel. Mostly, she stared at the kid with her hands on her hips and her eyebrows sunk low. It was almost a shame that nobody was trying to fight her. She would have known what to do if someone was trying to fight her.

"Well, Shina," she said after a couple minutes staring down at the girl. "I'm not saying you need to wake up *now*, but it would help us a lot if you *did*."

Silence.

Tazir let out a heavy sigh and got herself seated in the hammock next to hers. "All right, kid," she said, patting her on the shoulder. "I guess you can have another day."

Gently, softly as she could with her gnarled old hands, Tazir uncorked the water skin and put it to Shina's lips. They'd had to do this for her dying grandfather—you couldn't just pour the whole thing in, and you had to hold their head up and watch carefully to make sure they didn't start choking.

"That's it, girl," she murmured, smiling at the kid as she swallowed the water. "You're a tough little shit, you know that?"

She knew she had plenty of reasons not to show an

ounce of affection for this dipshit Windspeaker who'd lied to her, led her on some fool quest to sink the Dragon Ships, and then gotten her blown out to sea on short water and a shorter temper. But still, she couldn't help but feel some—some *admiration* for this sheltered little songbird. It took a lot of good, sailorly virtues to pull off a stunt like Shina had just done. Even if she did sleep for two days afterward.

Tazir figured it was because she was young. Young, weak, and trained from god knows what part of her infancy to rely on her teachers like a drooling melonhead who couldn't walk straight. Maybe if she spent some time around better people—strong people, people who valued fending for themselves—it wouldn't be so hard on her, this weird gift from a nasty, powerful old goddess.

"That's all I got for you now," Tazir said, brushing a drop of water from the girl's lower lip. For a moment, her hand lingered on Shina's face. Tazir snorted, stood up suddenly, and walked back over to the hatchway.

. . .

The sun was creeping down toward the horizon by the time the kid responded to anything at all—and that was almost slapping Tazir across the face when she tried to give her water.

"Fuh—fuh—" Shina's eyes flew open, and she bolted upright in the hammock.

"It's me, Tazir," she said, stepping back. "The Captain."

Shina shook her head and took a few steadying breaths, staring at Tazir. Then, she looked at her feet, shook her head, and leaned down to stretch her back.

"Where am I?" she asked. She got herself sitting with her legs dangling on the floor. "Did—are we—"

"We got out of Kuhon fine and dandy," Tazir said. "Thanks to you."

Shina's mouth hung open. "I—" Her cheeks darkened. "I didn't—" She sucked a long breath into her chest. "I didn't do what I was supposed to."

"Well, if you don't tell us what you were supposed to do," Tazir said, "then we won't be an inch the wiser." She handed the kid the water skin. "Here, drink up, but not much more than a cup—we never did get to Amasita's to refill our casks."

"Thank you," Shina said, reaching out for the skin. Like Tazir, she sipped it slowly, savoring the coolness as it washed down her throat. "Where are we?"

"About two days out from Moliki, the—" Tazir bit back her comment about the wind. The kid sounded like she had enough misplaced guilt on her shoulders already. "The water's not gone yet, but we're tight on it."

"I won't drink too much, then——"

"Nah." Tazir held her hand out to the proffered skin. "You need to keep your strength up."

"For what?" Shina's eyes narrowed as she sipped the water. "Are you going to turn me over to one of the Prefects?"

"Oh, right," Tazir said. "Talking to a Prefect about this fugitive who *paid me forty thousand qyda* to take her *up to the fucking long banks* no questions asked is *exactly* what I want to do on my day off."

Shina pursed her lips; her wide, dark eyes scanned Tazir's face.

"What, you think I'm so prim and proper that I count every fish?" Tazir rolled her eyes. "I wasn't hanging out in Shasa's looking for actual runaway brides."

"You're still a sailor," she said. "More likely than not, you'd rather drown me than give me some of your water."

"Drown you?" Tazir laughed. "Kid, I'm starting to like you. That stunt you pulled back there saved all our——"

"That wasn't *me*," Shina said. "I mean—it was *in* me, but——" Her mouth flapped open for a few moments before she shut her eyes and shook her head. "Where is the compass?" she asked.

"Should be hanging above your head with the rest of your shit," Tazir said. "You've been out cold for a couple of days."

"I couldn't—" She shook her head, rubbed her temples with her fingertips. Without another word, she turned around to untie the canvas sack where Chaqal had stuffed her shass set and the burning orb that Shina called a compass.

Tazir's eyebrows shot up when the kid pulled it out of the bag. Instead of flaming coral pink, the orange-sized sphere was chalky white. Shina stared at it intently, her lower lip caught between her two front teeth.

"I got this from the storm temple in Jepjep," she said. "It—it was in a jar, and the Windspeaker there told me to break it hard."

"Like you do," said Tazir with a smile.

"So I broke it," Shina continued, "and this was inside, and there were—these—they were like dark gulls, made of shadows and little bits of cloud." She looked up at Tazir. "There were five of them, and when I opened my mouth they all flew inside."

Tazir's eyebrows shot up. She nodded. "Huh."

"Aksa-auntie said they were storms. Too big for me to handle right now. I'm starting to think they might be too big for *anybody* to handle on their own." She took another sip of water and stared down at the compass. "I had—I mean, I needed to get us a strong wind, and I thought—" She stared down at her lap. "I could control the first one," she said. "It wasn't even hard."

"To be fair," Tazir said, "the Dragon Ships weren't attacking when—"

"It's not just the Dragon Ships," Shina said.

"Huh?"

Now Kodin was stirring in his hammock in the dark end of the bunks. "Hey," he murmured. "Can you two—"

"Shut up," Tazir said. "She's explaining her quest."

Kodin grunted and shifted again. "I wanna be on a quest," he said, sitting up. "Can I be on the quest?"

"Of course you're on the fucking quest," Tazir said. "You're the only one on this ship who can read."

"I can read," Shina offered.

"Yeah, but it's your damn quest. You're already on it."

Shina put her palms up. "All right," she said.

"That's what I thought." Tazir nodded. "So go on, what about the Dragon Ships and the storms and, I'm assuming, that freaky ol' ball you got on your lap."

Shina sucked on her teeth. "Well—umm, so. When the Dragon Ships hit Tash, they took our icon from the temple. It's—" She looked up at Tazir. "What do you know about the icon?"

Tazir shrugged. "You sacrifice babies to it?"

"No, we don't sac—" Shina clamped her lips shut. "All right. So, the icon was given to us a *long* time ago by one of the deep ocean spirits. A gift to the great Queen Mushaka'i after she brought down the Five Tall Witches.

You know that story?"

"A few versions," Tazir said.

"Fine, fine." Shina waved her hand. "The icon is a stone statue of a great big seahawk brooding on a nest, you know?"

"I've seen 'em," Kodin said.

"Yeah. So, after one of us at the school on Tash has studied hard enough, and learned to meditate like a grown-up and understand the weather patterns, we get presented to the icon. And that spirit—whose name I am not allowed to say before I go through this—judges you and sees if you're ready."

"All right," Tazir said. "Is this where the whole eyeball thing comes in?"

"Yeah," said the kid. "If you're ready, your new eyes will pop out of the icon like eggs, and they put you to sleep—" She rolled her eyes at the disgust on Tazir's face. "And when you wake up, it's as if—it's as if you're connected to the storms like never before."

"Uhh," Kodin said, "but doesn't it weaken—"

"I wasn't finished," Shina said. "It's—it lets you see the big patterns, and connect with the other Windspeakers. And they can see you too." She took a sip of water and looked at the ceiling for a few moments. "So, like, Papa Tu-huin off of Sapanji, a few years ago, came in, and they had to force him through the process." She grimaced. "But then when he had the stone eyes, when he would start to build a storm, the new Windspeakers assigned to him would take it apart as he put it together. A lot of work, but good practice."

Tazir nodded. She'd been on the fringes of one of the storms that son of a bitch had sent rolling up the Tahanas Isles, punishment for some Prefect's slight to one of his wives. "But now—"

"But now nobody can do anything," Shina said. "It's—you need to—the new eyes change you," she said. "Once you have them, you need them—and you need the icon."

"What," Kodin said. "Does it—control the eyes or something?"

"Kind of." Shina nodded. "We're not actually supposed to talk about how it works." She gave them a weak smile and sipped her water again. When she finished, she corked the skin and blinked slowly for a few moments. "I—ugh." She rubbed her forehead. "I don't want to be rude, but do we have any food left?"

"What do you want?" Tazir asked, turning around and stepping to the pantry. "We still have some fresh mangoes, a sack of dried ananas, and—"

"A mango would be wonderful," said Shina. She got to her feet, wobbling a little bit as she stood. Tazir took a step toward her, but she put her hand up. "I'm fine."

"All right," Tazir replied.

As Kodin got out one of the still-green fruits they'd bought from the discount vendor in Jepjep, Chaqal started swearing in Kuri abovedecks.

"Cap, I need you up here," she called down.

"Coming," Tazir said. "Kodin, we might need you too."

Shina looked for somewhere to set her mango. "I can—"

"Nah, girl," Kodin said. "You stay here and get feeling better."

Shina turned the corners of her mouth down and grumbled something as she slumped back into the hammock. Kodin rolled his eyes and followed Tazir up the ladder into the blustery sunlight abovedecks.

Chaqal was at the boom, glaring at the sail while she fiddled around for an angle that worked. "I think we need to adjust the starboard tension again," she said. "The wind shifted back."

"Are you serious?" Tazir said.

"I mean, we can just beat into it for however long it takes to switch back again," she said, "but that's gonna be thirsty work."

"May as well pull line while we're all awake," said Kodin.

As the three of them got to work shifting the belly to

the other side of the sail, Tazir noticed a familiar black puffball sticking out of the hatch. Shina didn't say a word as she watched, sucking on her mango.

"Go back to bed," Chaqal yelled when she noticed her. "You can't—"

"What's our speed?" Shina asked.

"Not great," Tazir snapped. "And it won't get better until we fix this—Kodin, I got my end." She gripped the rope and held it tight over one shoulder.

Shina wiped her mouth on the back of her hand and looked up at the sail, her eyebrows furrowed. "How far are we from the next port?"

"I would call it eighty miles," said Tazir. "Which, at the rate we're going, is looking to be about two days' time."

Shina tore the last chunk of mango from the pit and swallowed it. "How much fruit do we have?" she asked.

"We've got nine more of those mangoes," said Chaqal.

"If I eat another, I can try and call up another wind for us."

"*Now* she offers," Tazir said.

"Is that a good idea?" Kodin asked, his eyes intent on the knot he was finishing. "All right, I'm tied down."

Tazir threaded her end of the rope through its winch and held it tight with one hand while she wound it with the other. "Got it!"

"I've done it before," Shina said.

Kodin gave her a good long gaze with his mouth turned down and his brows knit together. "You know, that's a mighty duty you're taking on there."

The kid's mouth trembled. It occurred to Tazir that Shina probably knew that duty more deeply than anyone else on the boat.

"Yep," Shina said. She managed a brave smile for Tazir and Kodin.

There being no further objections to her plan, the kid retreated belowdecks to try to get herself in storm-spitting condition. By the time she came back up, the wind had switched twice, and the *Giggling Goat* was only a little bit closer to the next port. Tazir wasn't sure about Kodin, but she was glad to see the Windspeaker climbing up on deck, a watchful Chaqal at her back. How many times, she wondered, had she glanced back to check up on her, made sure there were no worrisome noises coming from the hatchway?

"Hey, kid," Tazir called. "You ready for some easy work?"

Shina smiled weakly. Her bony hands were curled into fists. "I think so."

"Well," Tazir said, "not being a Stormcaller myself, I guess I don't know where to start." She waved her hand around the ship deck. "I'll leave this job to you."

"Thanks," Shina muttered. She paced around for a few steps like a dog looking for somewhere to sleep, then got down on her knees. For a few minutes, nothing happened—Shina just knelt there, perfectly still, lips barely open, face and palms held up toward the sky.

Chaqal was staring, captivated by the lanky girl who had begun to rock back and forth a little like a tree in a stiff breeze. Kodin was glaring at her with his arms crossed, standing there all puffed up like he was ready to drown her if she tried anything funny. Tazir realized her fingernails were digging into her palms as she watched Shina work.

The girl's lower lip jerked down, and a breath shuddered into her rib cage like she was about to cry. Indeed, a sharp little gasp did emerge from her lips at the apex of it—but instead of sound, she exhaled that same strange, thick mist she'd vomited on the beach in Kuhon.

Except this time, the mist wasn't colored a thick leaden grey. It was pearly—kind of blue, kind of, oh, maybe yellow, even—and though it was thick as molasses, it was somehow as clear as glass. Tazir watched as it drifted out from Shina's murmuring lips, across the air above the deck, and then up toward the sky. She was struck by how beautiful it was, the whole storm-spitting thing. Why would you want to lock up a talent like that?

Why would you want to mutilate it and brainwash it until it was domesticated?

"Uhh—" Kodin was staring not at the mist, but at the sail. It had gone completely limp, as had the air around the *Giggling Goat.*

Tazir felt her fingernails dig into her palm. When she looked at Shina, the mist had disappeared.

"Ohh?" Chaqal pointed at the sail. "Maybe—"

Tazir saw it, too. A new wind—a *better* wind—was filling the striped canvas. The belly they had so carefully placed with rope tension was now useless—actually, worse than that. "Hey, Kodin!"

"Yeah."

Without another word between them, Tazir and her first mate went about lining up the sail and the wind. Now and then their eyes would meet, and they'd look at Shina, and they'd look at each other, and then they'd look as far away from each other as they could. This was weird.

Once the sail was angled as efficiently as they could get it, Kodin went to the stern to check their speed. Shina had opened her eyes again; she was leaning back on the heels of her hands and breathing heavy, as though she'd just run a race.

She looked up at Tazir and gave her a faint, shaky smile. "I'll be fine in a moment," she said. "That should—that should help us out a little bit."

"I'd say," Tazir said. "Hey, what's our speed?"

"I need a few minutes to be sure," Kodin said, "but we've picked up—we're doing maybe ten or twelve knots right now."

"Holy shit," Tazir muttered. She looked at the kid, sitting stoically on the deck as if she hadn't done a thing.

"The wind should hold for several days," Shina said as she stood. She wobbled, took a deep breath, and went to the railing. Her smile had faded into a tight-jawed stare at the horizon. "Yeah," she said, as if to herself. "A few days, at least."

• • •

After only half a day, Tazir spotted land. The island of Moliki was a low, wooded collection of hills that sat to one side of a reef where the locals dove for spiny lobsters. Just the thought of one of those succulent sons of bitches, all steamed up on top of rice with coconut sauce hot enough to make your eyes bleed from three feet away, was enough to get Tazir licking her lips.

"That's a welcome sight," Kodin said, pointing toward the horizon.

"No shit," Tazir replied. "You got a glass?" Though she had seen Shina spit the wind with her own eyes, she still didn't quite believe that she was already looking at

Moliki.

"Here." Kodin handed her the intricately carved spyglass he carried around his neck.

"Thanks." Tazir put the glass to her eye and turned the handle until the city came into—that couldn't be right. She adjusted the lens again, but—she *had* been in focus.

"What's wrong?"

"Nothing." Tazir handed the spyglass back to Kodin. Her eyes were wide, and her lips were hanging open. "Or at least," she murmured, "nothing that the kid needs to see just yet."

Chapter 6

Shina had first noticed the silence when she'd been stretching the wind out, past Moliki and northward toward the long banks. It wasn't unusual, of course, for a small port to be a little quiet on a hot afternoon. Shina hadn't believed that it was truly *silent*—she wasn't so refined in wind-spitting that she never got a mistaken impression.

As it turned out, silence was an understatement.

"I think most everybody got to safety," the Captain said, giving her a smile. "I've waited out a hurricane here myself—they have big, smooth roads and plenty of hills to shelter in."

Shina said nothing and kept staring out at what was left of Moliki.

The storm must have hit them straight behind from the south, and suddenly. The wooden wreckage of ships made a tangled line on the shore of the harbor, dotted with bodies swelling in the sun. Although the stone foundations of some of the buildings still stood, nearly every wooden building had been smashed by a storm surge.

And she'd done it all herself.

A flash of motion on the beach caught her eye. An old woman was tearing apart a pile of broken timbers, her movements desperate and erratic. Now and then, she would pause in her work to clutch at her face, and her wails carried across the harbor.

There were others, too, searching for evidence of hope in the wreckage of their homes. It was one thing to be hit by a natural storm, or a storm called up by somebody trained and stone-eyed. Those storms—they followed rules, or at least existed within the same limits as storms that followed rules.

I did this, she thought to herself. She'd hated wild Windspeakers in school—the ones who didn't want to be there, who thought they had some kind of right to do as they pleased with the weather. Some of them just didn't know what a storm could do if you spat it out and left it.

Others didn't *care.* They were worse—and now Shina might as well be among them. *Not my problem,* they'd say. *Build your houses a little stronger, and it won't be yours either.*

"You saved our lives," the Captain said softly. She put one of her big, rough hands on Shina's shoulder and squeezed.

Shina opened her mouth, but couldn't think of a

word that would hold her horror. How many lives had she taken? How many more livelihoods—livelihoods she had sworn to protect—had she dashed against the rocks without a single thought?

She had to turn away. A sob rose in her chest, but she bit it back down. Who was *she* to cry over this city? Who was *she* to mourn people whose lives hadn't even occurred to her when she'd spit that storm back in Kuhon?

The Captain patted her gently on the back. Shina flinched at the touch, but said nothing. "It's gonna be fine," she said. "It's not your fault."

Shina's mouth hung open. "How?" she said, in a voice that squeaked and whined.

"You did what you had to," the Captain replied. "You didn't—you didn't mean to do all this."

"But I didn't think to avoid it, either." Shina swallowed, shook her head. "Same outcome. Same thing."

The Captain gave her a weird look and opened her mouth, but shut it again and turned her eyes back to the shore. The two of them stood there in silence as the Captain moored the *Giggling Goat* at what was left of a short dock near the northern rim of the harbor. The crew disembarked with stony faces and hushed voices—fitting for visitors of the dead.

"There's a fresh spring not far from here," said the Captain, gesturing to the south. Without comment, the crew followed her into the worst of the destruction.

The main street of town was strewn with debris. A dog was harassing some chickens in the fractured remains of a butcher's shop. Overripe fruits had washed out of their seller's stall and lodged themselves in all kinds of strange places. A woman with long locked hair lay half-buried in splintered wood, her filmy eyes barely cracked open in the sun.

Shina stumbled, then sank to her knees. This was all too much—too much to even understand. The awful images swirled around her head, vivid before her eyes even after she had covered her face and begun weeping. There was no holding the tears back anymore. Her grief surged out of her chest in huge grey waves, salty and painful.

"It should have been someone else," she moaned into her damp palms. "Anyone else, anyone *better*—"

"Hey, now," the Captain said, at her side once again. "You did what you had to."

"But I did it *wrong*," Shina said.

Tazir put a hand beneath her arm and drew Shina to her feet. "Nah," she said. "Whoever—whoever did the thing before the storm went in your stomach. *They* might have screwed up, but you—you're innocent." She took Shina by the hand and led her forward. "You didn't have a choice in this."

Ahead of them, Kodin and Chaqal were looking

through the rubble, lifting boards and logs and stones, calling for people who'd been trapped.

"They must've been in a hurry," Kodin called back, "but I think most of them got out."

From down the beach, a fresh wail of grief confirmed his guess. Shina shut her eyes and took a deep breath. *I'm the last Windspeaker,* she reminded herself. *I'm the best option we have.*

A man's voice came from uphill, although they couldn't see where. "Hey!" he was calling. "Hey! Hey, over here!"

The Captain and Kodin looked around, blinking. The Captain chewed on her lip.

"Hey!" the voice repeated. Another voice asked something in a dialect Shina didn't understand.

"There, coming toward the harbor mouth!" replied the first. "Ships!"

The Captain looked back at Shina and raised her eyebrows. From where they were, what was left of the marketplace blocked the view of the harbor.

"Come on," Shina murmured to Tazir. "I need to get back to the ship." She pulled her hand from the Captain's grip and ran toward the ruin. Her stomach felt like she'd just swallowed a big gulp of air—or maybe a handful of Galinese death chiles. "I forgot my—"

When they rounded the corner, they could see those

red-striped sails, those painted dragons.

"—compass."

For a few moments, Shina and Tazir watched the almost silent advance of the Dragon Ships. There were three this time. One of them—going by the fire kindling in Shina's stomach, at least—had the icon on board.

"I need to eat," Shina said. She turned around and started searching the street for something that wasn't too badly damaged. Wedged in a wrecked doorframe, she found a mango that was just beginning to rot. With shaking fingers, she peeled off the spoiled part and devoured it like she hadn't eaten in weeks. Her stomach ached more and more with every bite—by the end, it was a chore to chew the oversweet pulp and get it down her throat.

"Here," Tazir said, tossing her some browning bananas she'd found beneath an overturned rowboat.

"Go get Chaqal and Kodin," Shina replied. She scanned the ruined city for a good place to sit. "Get to safety."

Tazir nodded. "And you?" she asked.

Shina kicked some debris off of a flat stone slab. "I'll be fine," she said through a mouthful of fruit.

"You'll be fine?" The Captain glared at her. "You'll be—dammit, Shina, you passed out last time!"

"This is my duty," Shina replied.

"That's great!" Tazir said. "It's *my* duty to make sure my—*you* don't get killed trying to save us."

Shina met the Captain's eyes. She was standing all puffed up with her fists balled and her shoulders drawn up on her neck. "Your what?" she said.

"Never mind," Tazir said. She gritted her teeth and turned to leave.

"If you and Chaqal want to come back for me," Shina called, "I won't be able to stop you."

Tazir stopped, turned back. She flashed a smile at Shina before running off to find Chaqal and Kodin.

The ships were close enough that Shina could hear the monstrous heartbeat of the oar drums thumping across the water. They were coming in slow—cautiously, even, judging by their formation.

Shina stuffed half a banana in her mouth and forced herself to swallow, kneading at her throat and shutting her eyes. Her gut was roiling, burning, starting to swell with the pressure of the storm building inside it—but she couldn't let it out. Not yet.

She sat down with her legs crossed and shut her eyes. As her chest began to rise and fall in rhythm with the waves, she could start to feel the weather in her body. The harbor was bathed in the wind she'd called the day before—but here, the air was a little slacker. Spent. Shina frowned as it filled her lungs, and when she exhaled she cast her mind out as far as it would go along the filaments of herself that remained in the wind.

Now, she could see clearer. Well, she couldn't really *see,* but that was the best she could explain what she was doing. The wind wasn't weak, she realized. It was slow, straining against something in its way.

The storm in her belly grew. It wouldn't be long, now; whoever had first designed it had made it more than capable of bursting out of her body the hard way.

Shina could feel it more distinctly now—the huge, wet, dark mass struggling with her wind. It rumbled and groaned, weakened in the last few hours but still angry, ready to lash out with surging waves and stinging salt spray. When Shina reached out for it, the storm growled and tightened; several mammoth waves raced through the sea around it.

She had not created this.

Somewhere behind her, back on Moliki, a ripple of pain went through her body. Shina struggled to stay focused on her storm. It would take a huge, rapid wind to move a wild storm like this, and it would take a wild storm like this to dash the hollow hulls of the Dragon Ships against the rocks of Moliki Harbor.

Come out, she whispered to the storm inside her. *Come out here and make a friend.*

She could tell that her forehead had smacked against

stone—and then her whole body smacked against something else. She kept her focus on the storm. *Come out,* she said.

As a dark, foaming wind shook the sea around the wild storm, Shina was vaguely aware that her body was seizing up and thrashing. She hoped the Captain really had returned for her.

Come back, she whispered, stroking the storm that was now taking shape on the clear blue sea. It was swirling around with the wild storm, testing its boundaries, but not yet pushing it where she wanted it to go. She tugged on it, struggled with it, pleaded with it—

But wouldn't it be easier, she thought, if she just spat out the last storm she had in her stomach?

All things considered, it wasn't the wisest idea in the world. She had no way of knowing whether her body was safe or not, and there was a good chance she'd drown along with the raiders who came in the Dragon Ships. But what was one more corpse among the masses of innocent people she'd already drowned? What was her own safety compared to the safety of the thousands who lived under the threat of the Dragon Ships? What was the point of trying to stay alive if it meant giving up the *one chance* she had at making it bearable to live with her powers?

She had to strain to call this one out. For a frozen

moment, she felt her focus slipping—terrified, she jolted herself back into her task. This wind did not want to go. It did not want to leave her mouth. It did not want to press its bulk against the mass of hissing cloud and spray in front of it. Even when Shina had drawn the headwind to the side, she had to use every ounce of energy she had left to push this mass of cloud back toward Moliki.

She stayed conscious until it was almost in the harbor mouth.

Chapter 7

By the time she was maybe twenty or twenty-five, Tazir had learned that she needed to stop claiming she'd seen every type of storm they could stir up for the Jihiri Islands. There was always something bigger, nastier, and scarier waiting to come in from the east, and there was always something new that could go wrong while you tried to weather it.

But this—holy shit. Holy *shit*.

She'd seen smooth-sided banks of clouds like that before, back when she was still a kid working the sail on the *Sleeping Snake*. They'd run like hell from a wild hurricane while every Windspeaker in the islands worked like a mule to divert it from the most populated ports. Even now, flight was her general policy when clouds stood tall over the water and the air billowed so fast it made your ears pop.

It was Kodin's policy, too.

"Damn you, Captain!" he roared after her. He was too big and stiff-kneed to chase her through the wreckage that lay between the tree line and the beach, but he was making a good try at it. "I did *not* plan on dying on this trip!"

"Then get back to the trees!"

"Not without you, I won't." He was huffing and puffing, unused to hurrying any farther than fifty feet.

Tazir wasn't much better, but she kept going. The sand sucked at her feet, and the effort tied her stomach into a painful knot. Up ahead, Chaqal darted like a spider between flotsam and jetsam and rocky parts, using her arms as much as her feet. She was almost to the edge of town.

"Leave her!" Kodin shouted. "Get back here, both of you!"

"No!" screamed Tazir. "We have to get her out!"

"What is *wrong* with you?"

It was a good question. The wind-polished hulk of the storm was racing toward Moliki on a mighty wind that stung Tazir's eyes and sent smaller pieces of rubble flying past her. It had begun to rain, thick droplets that smacked hard against her bare skin. Beneath the cloud, Tazir couldn't really see *anything*, but that itself was certainly something to look at. You couldn't really tell where the storm cloud began and the sea spray ended.

"Hurry!" Chaqal called, turning around to wave frantically at Tazir. "They're here!"

Tazir stopped, her eyes wide and her nostrils flared.

She couldn't hear the beat of the oar drums anymore, not over the wind. "What do you mean they're *here*?"

But Chaqal was already gone, leaping over a pile of splintered wood and canvas that might have been someone's house once upon a time.

"Really?" Tazir yelled after her. *"Really?"*

Once she got to the edge of town, it was easier going. Tazir was neither fast nor young, but *damn* did firm ground make a difference beneath her feet. She followed Chaqal through the maze of ruined houses on the edge of town, jumping over boards and bodies and gasping for air and—

She ran right into her quartermaster, nearly knocking them both to the ground.

"What the *shit*," Tazir grumbled. "You don't—"

And then she saw why Chaqal had stopped.

The stories about the Dragon Ships were like the stories about the giant marlin your cousin Bua'ka caught off Tobagawa last year. Giant, skinless warriors with three eyes or six legs; fire mages who could call a lightning bolt down with the snap of a finger; grotesque hybrids of humans and beasts that nobody had seen before—honestly, Tazir could listen to that shit until the sun came up.

But there was a reason the stories went that way. Nobody wanted to hear about a bunch of armored warriors—most of them around Kodin's size—pouring out of a ship like it was a damned anthill. This wasn't a sight to entertain you and keep your ass on a barstool for one more round. This was a sight to make you run.

"They're gonna find her," Chaqal said. "Come on!"

"Hey, now—"

But her quartermaster had already taken off, her braid whipping in the wind as she raced toward the square where Tazir had left Shina. The warriors gathered on the beach—one of them, Tazir could see, was wearing a high metal helmet with a grotesque face carved on it. He was pointing up at the city and arguing with a man who held his helmet at his hip.

Good. Let them argue instead of getting the hell out of this storm. The longer they did *that*—

A roar—like thunder, maybe? Or a great wave? Or—oh, shit, that was one of those fireballs they'd been lobbing out at Kuhon, wasn't it? A swath of the north end of town lit up in flames, and Tazir prayed they weren't preparing another blast.

"Shina!" Chaqal screamed, picking up her frantic pace even more as she neared the marketplace. "Oh, no—"

Now, Tazir could see the kid—and her heart skipped when she realized that she was lying on the hard ground, her face bruised and bloodied and her body convulsing like she had a bad fever.

She still wasn't fast or young, but she made a good effort at catching up to Chaqal when she saw that.

"Hurry!" called her quartermaster, who was kneeling down by the kid's unconscious body. "She's—oh, she's in a bad way, Cap!"

"I can see that," said Tazir. Her breath came in ragged gulps. The flames had never been far off, and they weren't getting any farther.

"We've got to *do* something!"

"Like this?" Tazir might not have been much of a runner, but you didn't stay married to Mati Yukali for four and a half years without learning to hoist a passed-out bitch up on your shoulders.

She grunted as she got a firm grip on the kid's arm. Shina was thrashing real good now, her eyes flickering open and closed with the eyeballs rolled almost all the way back into her head.

"Should we stick something in her mouth?" said Chaqal.

"Will that help?"

"I don't know!" her quartermaster squeaked. There were tears in her eyes, and her lip trembled.

"All right, all right—let's get out of here," said Tazir. "Help me drag her."

Chaqal put an arm under Shina's shoulders, and the two of them sped back through the wreckage of Moliki.

Behind them, Tazir heard another thunderclap, another roar of flame and smoke—and shouting. Were the raiders shouting at them?

"Hurry!" Chaqal said.

"I'm hurrying!" Tazir was wheezing from keeping up with the younger woman. Shina swung between them, her body twisting and her lips murmuring formless sounds. The wind had picked up, and brought with it a grey haze of salt spray that chilled the skin and put fear in the bones.

Kodin was already on the boat by the time the three of them made it to the beach. He grabbed Shina by the shoulders and hauled her up into the *Giggling Goat* so Tazir and Chaqal could crawl up the side.

Despite the driving wind and the freezing spray, the sea was weirdly calm. Tazir didn't have time to ponder why. She and Kodin didn't waste half a second getting the *Giggling Goat* the hell off its moorings and away from the harbor—there was no sense in waiting for the warriors from the Dragon Ships to take notice of them.

"Here it comes!" yelled Kodin as the oncoming storm sucked all the light out of the sky around them.

"No shit!" Tazir yelled back.

They said nothing else for a minute or two as they sailed the *Giggling Goat* as far east as they could as fast as they could. Whatever Shina was doing, she wasn't doing it to the east: east was good. East was—

Tazir felt the deck shift under her as the ocean rose up beneath the *Giggling Goat*.

She looked at Kodin. Kodin looked at her. For a moment, they were light on their feet, frozen in time, most *definitely* going to die. Behind Kodin, rolling down toward the harbor mouth, Tazir saw the peak of the wave rising high above the wreckage of Kuhon, a flat grey knife already edged with foam.

"Oh, fu—"

Everything went rolling across the deck as they came down the rear side. Tazir grabbed on to the railing and prayed to ancestors she hadn't thought about in years. She prepared herself for the smack of water against her skin, for the sea in her nose and her mouth and her eyes—but instead, she felt the deck rock and still beneath her.

For much too long, she clung to the railing with her eyes shut, ready to hit the water. She opened her left eye first, then her right, then blinked. The storm was still there, still spitting cold grey mist and bitter wind at her, but the water around the *Giggling Goat* was as calm as it had been before the wave struck.

She had never seen a rogue wave hit a town before. She guessed she'd always expected it to be—oh, she didn't know, maybe louder? More—with the spray and the wind and the crash of water on rock and wood, that kind of thing.

Maybe she was just too far away to really take it in, or maybe the air was hazy. Either way, all she could see was a hulk of grey water spilling over the shore of the harbor, spilling into town, picking up the flotsam and jetsam like hot broth picks up your noodles when you pour it in the kettle.

And then—when the wave retreated, pulling most of Moliki into the sea with it—*then* came the expected noise. The pops and cracks and groans all kind of mashed together with the sound of the water pouring back into the sea.

"Well," Kodin said. He was standing next to her now, staring at the destruction with his eyes wide and his jaw slack. "Fuck."

Tazir nodded, fishing in her sash for her pipe. "Too bad Shina's asleep," she said as she knocked out a wad of damp, stinking ash. "Be good for her to see she can get shit done when she needs to."

• • •

"She's saying something," a voice said—Kodin's voice. "She's—"

A coughing fit shook Shina's rib cage, startling her

back into consciousness. She was somewhere dark—damp, wet, noisy. It was raining. Her chest hurt. Her head hurt.

"Hey," she said. "Where—what, huh—"

"You're fine," Chaqal said. "We got you up here safe."

"What did—" Shina realized she was panting, gasping for air. She wondered if she'd drowned and been pumped back again. "Who—"

"You're back on the ship," Tazir said. "We got out before the storm hit, and it pissed out after that little display of yours."

"Huh?" Shina sat up. She was, indeed, belowdecks. "Display?"

"The big wave?" Chaqal asked. "The—you don't remember that?"

Shina stared ahead, blinking. "No," she said. "What—did I sink them?" she asked.

"Sink them?" Chaqal laughed. "Sure, you sunk them. There's nothing *left*."

A smile tugged at the corners of Shina's mouth. "Really?" she asked.

"Yeah," said Tazir, handing Shina a less rotten banana. "You wanna go up and see it?"

Shina had never wanted to be one of those people who gloat over the destruction they could do by calling up a storm. But, considering all that had happened, she wasn't too disgusted with herself for letting Kodin haul her up to the *Giggling Goat*'s top deck.

They were drifting across the harbor in a light wind that Shina did not recognize. You could still tell that the storm was there, an unnaturally heavy fog that hung around the wreckage of the port town and the trees of the jungle above it. But it had finally spent itself, finally found its target.

And it had destroyed it.

If you knew what to look for, you could tell the Dragon Ships had once floated these waters. Shreds of red-striped sail clung to pieces of wreckage; pale-skinned corpses mixed with the flotsam that had already lined the stricken harbor. To the south a little ways, the brightly painted remains of a carved dragon's head stuck out of a raft formed of rags and splinters.

Shina realized she was smiling—and she didn't really feel bad about it.

"Not bad, eh?" said the Captain.

Shina's smile went thin at the edges as she turned to face her. "I'm not sure what I did," she said.

"That makes two of us." Tazir lit her pipe and took a few long puffs. "We were trying to make it to the lee of the island when you picked the damn boat up fifty feet in the air. Heard this rumble like—like—" She waved her hands in a circle in front of her face. "Shit, girl, we didn't think there'd be anything left of the harbor."

"And you all got me out?" Shina looked behind her—the quartermaster hadn't yet come back on deck.

"Barely." Tazir puffed on her pipe.

Shina looked out at the deep grey water of the harbor, rippling quietly in the mist. This didn't feel real. She bit her tongue, but this wasn't some cruel prank her mind was playing on her. She'd sunk the Dragon Ships.

And the icon. She'd—she didn't really have a *plan* for the icon from here. She'd drowned the people who had it, and that was a start. But what now?

"How deep do you think this is?" she asked, watching a scrap of sail sink beneath the waves.

"I don't know," Tazir said. "Out here, I'd say ten fathoms. Up in the edges it gets down to about three at low tide."

Shina's face fell.

"What?"

"Oh, it's—" She cast her eyes over the harbor. "It's going to take days to find the icon."

"Wait, *what*?" Tazir took a step back.

"The icon," Shina said. "The statue I was telling you about."

"The one they rip out your eyeballs for!" Tazir looked Shina up and down. "You actually wanted to—"

"To bring it back," Shina said, nodding. "So we

can—so our elders can have their power back."

"So they can *rip the eyes out of your head*!" Tazir balled her hands into fists. "Are you—are you fuckin' serious?"

Shina stared at the Captain in silence. "Yes?"

"You're insane!"

"You—you saw what happened here," she said. "You saw how many people died because I couldn't—because we couldn't see the consequences of what we'd done."

"But it wasn't your faul—"

"I don't care whose *fault* it was!" Shina's voice came out louder than she expected. "All right? I don't *care* if *you* think I killed those people! It's not—"

"But look at the lives you saved," she said. "Look at *our* lives, kid!"

"Don't tell me whose lives to look at, Captain," Shina said. "Not until innocent people are dead because of something *you* did."

"I'll tell you anything I like," said the Captain. "Probably had a few people shit themselves to death after eating my day-old shrimp by now. Not my fuckin' fault they bought it, and it's not your fuckin' fault that some of those people were literally too stupid to come in out of the rain."

Shina blinked. "You sell day-old shrimp?"

"How, after going through all of this, are you still Miss High and Mighty?" Tazir said. "How do you still have this—this—"

"This *duty*," Shina said. "I have a duty."

"You have a problem in your head!" Tazir roared, advancing on her. Shina cowered back against the ship's railing—she knew there was no way on earth she could take this woman in a fight. "These priests and magicians went and brainwashed you," Tazir continued, "until you didn't have a lick of common sense left!"

"They didn't," Shina said, grabbing the railing.

"Well, I'll tell you what else," Tazir said. "They're not gonna do it again." She reached forward to grab Shina's arm.

"Hey!" Shina jerked away. "What are you trying to—"

"I'm trying to get you down below," Tazir said, "so you can take a damn nap until you come to your senses."

Chaqal had come up through the hatchway. "Captain—"

"She's trying to go diving into the harbor!" Tazir snapped back. "After that *fucking* statue—"

"Well, it's not out here," Chaqal said. "It would be closer—"

"That's not the fucking point!" Tazir rounded on her quartermaster. "If you think I'm gonna let this crazy goddamn bitch—"

Shina was too tired for this. Her eyelids were too

heavy, and her knees were too weak. All she wanted to do was go down below, to go to bed and try to forget that any of this had happened.

She turned around and dove into the harbor.

Chapter 8

"Rum and lime for both of us," Tazir said, pulling up a stool. "Double strong."

"You pay cash," the barmaid said. She was a tall, slender thing, dark as midnight, with a great ball of black hair tied back from her forehead with a red silken scarf.

Tazir glared at her as she fished in her purse for a few dakki. "Do we need a bath that bad?" she said.

Kodin chuckled next to her, but the barmaid's face stayed placid as she plunked a pair of clay cups down on the table. "It's a cash bar," she said. "You pay cash."

Tazir set the coins down on the bar with a thunk. "I got cash," she said. "I ain't poor again just yet."

She was close, though. Close enough that Leyo was sleeping in his hammock tonight instead of drinking with them on their last evening in Humma. Close enough that they were in Shasa's again, looking over the crowd of regulars with practiced eyes.

It wasn't as if she'd spent the money badly. Twenty-five thousand had gone to cover debts for her and Kodin and a dead friend of Kodin's and Tazir's twat ex-sister-in-law. Another ten thousand had gone into the *Laughing Dancer,* a younger and less complicated dhow with a rudder that didn't warp and need replacing every nine months.

"Hey," Kodin said, nodding toward the edge of the canopy. A young man with his hair in braids was standing there, smoking a pipe and surveying the crowd. He wore a dingy grey dhoti and weathered mat sandals; at his side was a bulging satchel that had been bleached by salt air.

He made eye contact with Tazir and tilted his jaw back. She raised her glass and cocked her head. He walked over, his young face exuding practiced calm.

"Excuse me," he said with a bow, "but I have a unique problem."

It was the same story that had been floating around Shasa's for twenty-five years. Cousin, marriage, running away. Said he had a side girl, she worked the docks in Moliki, could get him a job with her crate crew.

Tazir doubted they'd rebuilt Moliki enough in five years that they had stevedores on the docks, but she took him on anyway. He paid two hundred qyda up front, and he bought them their drinks for the rest of the night. He was funny, he was cute, and he knew a thing or two about handling a later-model dhow. He wasn't even bad in bed for a kid his age.

• • •

Even with an entertaining passenger like that, the trip to Moliki was slow going and boring as hell. She told the kid—as she told every new acquaintance she made on that hop between islands—about the time she'd done the trip in three days with a wet-eyed weather witch in tow.

He smiled politely, and he nodded politely, and he shared his skin of rum politely, but Tazir could tell he didn't believe her. That was just as well. She could see her braids turning silver and her face drooping down her skull; she could feel better than anyone the creaking pain in her hip when she had to stand up too long. It wasn't unreasonable, she guessed, to assume that her mind was starting to go the way of her body.

The boy was gone as soon as they were tied into one of Moliki's slips. Two hundred qyda was enough to get them a nice little second-story room in the back of Bosso's, with a reed mat for all three of them and laundry service in the morning.

It was enough to get all three of them plenty of rum, too, but by the time the sun set Tazir had barely managed a mug of rum and lime.

"You're a lot of fun," remarked Leyo as he returned to

their table with fresh rounds for him and Kodin.

"Yeah?" Tazir took a sip of her drink. "Should've seen me a few years ago."

Leyo rolled his eyes.

"You still think we're lying," Kodin said.

"I don't think you're *lying*," said the new quartermaster. "I just think you might be—exaggerating a bit." He raised his eyebrows and took a big swallow of his rum. He was one of Kodin's kin, a strapping Tashi boy who'd been nineteen when Chaqal took off in the middle of the night.

"Well," Tazir grumbled, "no sense yelling at a deaf man."

"You want me to believe you?" Leyo pointed his finger at her. "Take me up to the temple."

"Go up there yourself," Tazir said. "I don't wanna see that girl again." Not after she'd gone back to her own prison. Definitely not after she'd subjected herself to that—that torture.

"You don't want me to catch you lying," Leyo replied.

"Hey," Kodin said. "You watch what you're saying to Tazir."

"Oh, come on," the quartermaster moaned. "You two have been blowing smoke at me for the last five years—"

"I'll go up there with you," Kodin said. "I ain't afraid of her now she's got her eyes taken out."

"What the *fuck*, Kodin?" Tazir slammed her cup down on the table.

"You saw what she did to this place," Kodin grumbled. "You wanna go see her, cousin?"

"Yeah." A broad grin stretched across Leyo's face. "I ain't afraid of no skinny blind girl."

"Show some respect," Tazir snapped. She growled at the two men as they stood up from the table. "Fuckin'—I gotta follow you, don't I?"

. . .

By the time they reached the storm temple, Tazir was leaning heavy on Leyo's shoulder. Her hip was screaming, and she dragged her leg as she hobbled up the hill.

"I can carry you," Kodin offered for the fourth or fifth time.

"Fuck you," Tazir snapped back.

The men let her keep dragging and hopskipping her way up to the temple. Like every other temple, it was really a compound surrounded by a spiked bamboo fence. There was a big mud hut in the middle, surrounded by half a dozen outbuildings where the Windspeakers and their staff lived.

A pair of women in yellow-and-blue robes were sweeping the courtyard, their hair and faces covered by brightly printed scarves. They looked up from their task when Tazir and the men opened the gate and came inside. One, tall and thin, went back to her task. The other, short and plump, stared at the visitors for a second before coming toward them.

"Captain Tazir?" she called—and that voice brought back a flood of memories.

"Chaqal?" Tazir blinked, pushed Leyo away, and started walking toward her on her own. "Holy sh—I mean—"

The woman tipped her head back and laughed. "Oh, my gods," Chaqal said. "I never thought I'd see you here!" She reached Tazir and clasped her in a hug that smelled of incense and chiles. "And you brought Kodin, and—" She looked at Leyo.

"We have to have a quartermaster," Tazir said.

"Yeah," said Chaqal. She looked at her feet.

"This is Leyo," Kodin said, clapping his cousin on the shoulder. "He doesn't believe us when we tell him about this place."

Chaqal stepped back. "Oh," she said.

Kodin looked her in the eye for a few quiet, awkward moments. "So, uh," he said. "Is she around?"

"Is *who* around?" Chaqal crossed her arms.

"You know," Kodin said. "The girl."

"*Who?*" said Chaqal.

"You know who I'm talking about," said Kodin, holding his palms out. "The Windspeaker. The one we—"

Chaqal shook her head. "Get out." She thumped the handle of her broom against the courtyard's packed clay. "You can't even say her *name*?"

"Come on," Tazir said quietly. "We just wanted to see how Shina's doing."

"Did you?" said Chaqal.

"Yeah," Tazir said.

Her old quartermaster stepped back, staring at her with narrowed eyes. Tazir couldn't see, but could picture the scrunched mouth underneath the veil.

"Fine," Chaqal said. "I'll take *you* back to the rectory. *They* can wait back here and think about their manners."

Tazir opened her mouth to protest as Chaqal turned on her heel and walked back toward the outbuildings, but she couldn't find a damn thing to say that wouldn't get her in deeper trouble.

"In here," Chaqal said, gesturing to the door of a small round hut. "We're having dinner—I was going to join her once I got chores finished."

Tazir paused in the threshold to take her shoes off. She noticed that Chaqal now went barefoot. "How long you been here?" she asked, almost under her breath.

"A while," Chaqal said.

"Since you left me?" Tazir set her shoes down and

looked her in the eye.

Chaqal slid her eyes away. "Yeah," she said. "Since I left you."

"Huh." Tazir nodded and took a deep breath as she followed Chaqal inside the hut.

"It's me," Chaqal said as she approached the table in the middle. Shina was sitting there, still lanky and baby-faced—as long as she was looking down. When she turned her face up, Tazir could see the bright green stones in her eye sockets.

"Tazir?" she said, perhaps blinking out of habit.

Tazir took a step back. "Y-yeah," she said. "How—"

"I heard your voice outside," she said, grinning. "And you smell like tobacco."

"Oh." Tazir took a deep breath and pressed her lips together. "Yeah," she said. "It's me."

"Good," Shina replied. "I've been hoping you'd come for a visit—sit down!" She gestured to her right, where a round cushion sat unoccupied in front of the table. "How was your trip up here?"

"It was smooth sailing," Tazir said as she shuffled over to the cushion. "You do a good job, I guess."

"I'm still only part-time," Shina replied. "Mathul-uncle does most of the work with the trade winds."

"Well, I'm sure you're plenty helpful," Tazir said. She couldn't take her eyes off those stones—and what kind of sick fuck had gotten her that pink hair scarf embroidered in matching green thread? "They treating you all right?"

"Oh, of course." Shina smiled. "I've been living here since the temple was rebuilt," she said. "But I went to Druhuk for the surgery."

"Mmh." Tazir tried to hide the disgust on her face from Chaqal, but she still earned a filthy look. "I see you got that."

"It's better now," Shina said. "I don't worry so much," she said. "About everything."

"Oh-h?" Tazir forced a smile on her face. "That's—that's good."

The smile faded from Shina's lips. "What do you want me to say?" she asked.

"I—I don't—it doesn't matter to me," Tazir said.

"It was painless, if you want to know," Shina said. "They were right about that—"

"But your *eyes*," Tazir blurted. "They took your *eyes*."

"They did," said Shina. She felt on the table for the teapot and an empty cup. "What did they take from you?" She carefully moved the teapot until its spout clinked against the cup's rim, and poured most of a cup of tea. She pushed it across the table to Tazir.

Tazir was staring in front of her. "What?" she asked.

"What did they take from you?" Shina repeated. "I spend my days studying storms, touching clouds, molding winds—for that, I gave up my eyes."

"I didn't give up shit," Tazir said. She picked up the tea and took a drink—it was far too hot to do that, but she refused to show a lick of pain. "And I'm doing what I want, too."

"I'm sure you are," Shina said.

The three of them sat in silence after that. Shina resumed popping stuffed olives into her mouth, and Chaqal poured herself a bowl of fish stew. She had pushed her veil back to reveal her long, dark hair, and she avoided Tazir's gaze.

Suddenly, a bubble of anger welled in Tazir's chest. "Fuck this," she growled, standing up and sending the cushion flying behind her. "You two wanna spend the rest of your lives in this creepy eyeball-gouging weather-cult town?" she said. "You go ahead and—*fuck*!" She tumbled as her hip seized up, gritted her teeth, and staggered to the doorway.

"Captain!" Chaqal cried out. She hopped up and ran to Tazir, who was steadying herself and trying to ignore the pain shooting up her back.

"Get away from me," she growled.

"Captain—"

Tazir shoved Chaqal back. "I said, *get away* from me," she said. She took a deep breath and began hobbling out of the hut, back toward her crew. "And *fuck* your tea and olives."

. . .

Tazir lay there on the reed mat until the sun was high overhead. *I can get up,* she told herself. *I'm just a little too tired for that shit right now.*

Tazir was starting to get used to mornings like these. She'd lie there for—for however long she was allowed to, depending on the circumstances, and then she'd hobble over to her knapsack for a dose of poppy juice. She'd stretch, she'd curse, she'd smoke some hash, and eventually she'd get herself dressed.

But this morning, there was nothing there for her to sip or smoke.

"What the hell?" Tazir said, staring at the empty room around her. There were no knapsacks, no rum jugs, no piles of clothes left behind by her crew. "What the *hell*?"

She staggered down the stairs in her trousers with her tits flopping on her belly. "Kodin!" she yelled. "Kodin N'jakama, where the *fuck* are you—hey, you!" She pointed at a girl of ten or twelve, pushing a cart of laundry down the hallway. "You see a big guy in locks and a skinny kid with a sun tattooed on his right shoulder?"

The girl blinked. "This morning?" she said.

"Yeah, this morning." Tazir puffed up her chest and glared at the girl.

"Yeah," the girl said, staring at her feet. "They paid the bill on room twenty-two and took off. Said they had to be out by sunrise."

Tazir took a step back and held on to a post for balance. She took one deep breath, then another.

"Hey, were you with them?" said the girl. "I think they left a note with my pa at the front desk."

• • •

"—and if you agree to the terms, I can have the value of the ship paid back to you within six years," the clerk said. He was a short, round man with round spectacles balanced on his short, round nose. He wore a clean blue kaftan and a matching turban; his face grew graver and graver as he read the note from Kodin.

"I know you liked that girl, and I know it was hard on you when Chaqal left, but I told you before I don't want anything to do with the Windspeakers." The clerk frowned. "We can't stay in business if we scare a new quartermaster off every six months."

"He says, as he *ditches his Captain* in Moliki!"

"Madam, please, I am just reading the letter." The clerk looked up at her with wide eyes and a weak smile.

"Do you want me to go on?"

"Sure." Tazir sighed. She rested her face in her hands, her elbows on the counter.

The clerk adjusted his spectacles. "I expect you to be angry," he said, "but I also think that this is best for all of us. Please try to understand why we are doing this, and please take care of yourself until we return." He cleared his throat. "I hope that when we meet again, we can talk this out and come up with a contract on the boat that is fair to both of us. Yours in business and in friendship, Kodin N'jakama."

Tazir shut her eyes and sucked in a breath. "Son of a bitch," she hissed.

"He—he left you with a significant sum," the clerk pointed out, pushing a bulging leather purse toward her. "And he paid your board and laundry in full for the next month." His eyes flickered to the shelf of ceramic cat figurines on the wall beside him. "I—I urge you to please be peaceful with a humble messenger, ma'am."

Tazir nodded, pressing her mouth flat. "Yeah," she said, turning around with a jerk. "I don't beat on old men."

. . .

She sat at the empty slip for hours, her trousers hiked up

to her knees and her legs dangling in the water. Little fish had begun to investigate, tickling her ankles and darting away when she moved her toes.

The jug of rum was almost empty, and the heat of the day had made it sickeningly warm. Tazir drank it anyway. It went well with the lonely, hollow bitterness that already filled her gut.

"You told me, once, that you were afraid he'd leave you like this," said a familiar voice behind her.

"Yeah?" Tazir kept staring out to sea, trying to guess which one of the bright painted sails in the distance belonged to the *Laughing Dancer*. "Guess I was right," she said.

Chaqal's bare feet made quiet sticky sounds on the dock as she stepped closer to Tazir. "Sorry about last night," she said.

Tazir took a sip of the rum. "No, you're not."

Chaqal grunted. "I get sick of it," she said. "People coming to—to stare."

"Yeah?" Tazir said. "Maybe you shouldn't work at a storm temple."

Chaqal made an irritated noise in the back of her throat. "Doesn't it get exhausting?" she asked. "Being personally responsible for everything that happens to you?"

"That's life, sweetheart," Tazir said. She took a long

swig on the rum jug and winced as she choked it down. It wasn't that long until she could go back to bed and feel like a reasonable person. "We set our own courses, and we don't get to bitch about them when they turn out to be shitty."

"If you say so," Chaqal said. She leaned down for a moment; Tazir turned to see what she had set down on the dock next to her. It was a walking stick. A nice walking stick, yeah, carved out of dark-stained wood with carved fish swimming in a spiral up its length, but still—

"What the fuck is this?" Tazir said.

"It's a gift," Chaqal said. "People give them to each other all the time and barely ever die."

"Well, fuck your gift," Tazir said.

"Shina warned me you wouldn't like it," Chaqal said. She snorted. "Whatever," she said. "You're gonna go moon-eye crazy after a couple months sitting around on pension."

"So?"

"So, I'll ease up on dusting the shrine until then," Chaqal said. "Gotta leave some work for you to do."

Tazir snorted and drained her rum. When the last drop had burned down her throat, she smashed the jug against the dock.

Chaqal said nothing—and indeed, by the time Tazir was curious enough to turn around, she saw her old lover trudging down the dock with her head hung low.

"Dammit," Tazir grumbled, watching the blue-and-yellow figure grow smaller and less distinct. A memory crossed her mind—Shina, all those years ago, curled up on her mat on the deck and muttering. *The last one,* she used to whine in her sleep. *I'm the last one.*

"Dammit," she said again. Her hip protested as loud as it could as she tried to stand up.

"Dammit!" she yelled, thumping her fist on the dock. She glared at the walking stick as she picked it up. "Dammit, dammit, *dammit,*" she growled.

As she jerked herself to her feet, she could see that Chaqal had stopped and turned around to watch her.

"Hey!" Tazir yelled as she limped down the dock. She didn't want to admit how much faster she was, leaning on that damned stick. "The kid doesn't hear a fucking word about this. You hear me?"

Chaqal nodded at Tazir and went walking back toward town, her robes trailing in the dust behind her.

About the Author

Emily Foster graduated from the University of Northern Colorado in 2012 with a bachelor's degree in English. She has written and published a variety of work ranging from abstract poetry to Supreme Court briefs. However, her real passion is for fantasy fiction inspired by the unforgiving landscapes of her home in rural Colorado and the rugged people who live there. She is concerned that if she lists any pets or family members in her biography, it will somehow cause more of them to appear in her home.

TOR·COM

Science fiction. Fantasy.
The universe.
And related subjects.

*

More than just a publisher's website, Tor.com is a venue for **original fiction, comics,** and **discussion** of the entire field of SF and fantasy, in all media and from all sources. Visit our site today—and join the conversation yourself.